THE
BETRAYAL
OF
LEE

THE
BETRAYAL
OF
LEE

Jennifer Janell

CONTENTS

Prologue.. xi

Chapter 1   Baby Blues 1
Chapter 2   After Effects....................................14
Chapter 3   The New Normal 23
Chapter 4   Planning for Disaster 34
Chapter 5   Failed Seduction 45
Chapter 6   Sisterly Bond................................51
Chapter 7   What Comes Around........................ 59
Chapter 8   Confrontations 70
Chapter 9   Secret Rivalry 76
Chapter 10   Emotionless Connections...................... 90
Chapter 11   Marriage Recovery........................ 99
Chapter 12   Dangerous Confessions......................105
Chapter 13   Back to Normal 110
Chapter 14   The Deception Game 115
Chapter 15   Final Decisions 122

Epilogue... 129
Letter From The Author................................133

ACKNOWLEDGEMENTS

I would like to thank my readers and everyone that supported me as a new author. Special thanks to Khloe's Thoughts Editing Services for editing, and Monique Mensah for coaching me and getting another book into readers' hands. I look forward to more success with all of you at my side.

DEDICATION

This book is dedicated to all who joined Leesha's journey and found a little of themselves along the way.

~Jennifer Janell

"In whatever you face be strong, be happy, and be present. There is no need to know or fix everything because in the end, it's really not that serious. Have fun, love, live, and remember your worth."

~Johnathon

PROLOGUE

"Karl really! Again! I'm so sick of this shit. What is the point in paying supervisors, a foreman, and architect if you always gotta be there. I'm tired, the girls are running around here like maniacs, and you're leaving!"

"It's my job, my family's business! I'm sick of you always complaining. This needy shit is driving me up the fucking wall!"

"Needy? Is that what I am? Or am I a realist and see straight through your late nights and extended work weeks? What are you really doing out there?"

"Here we go; there she is – insecure Leesha, I was wondering when you were going to show up." His words stung. Karl had been almost unrecognizable the last few weeks. I knew the stress of the new subdivision the company was working on was weighing on him, so once again I was willing to overlook the inconsiderate comment. That *insecure* insult had become his go-to lately, which did something to me. It was hard enough being a full-figured Black woman, married to a handsome successful white man, but calling me insecure was pretty low in my opinion. This was a reminder of my verbally abusive dad; the first man that ruined my confidence who happened to be white. So, this situation fucked with me on so many levels.

"It's not about being insecure, it's about wanting my husband to put me and his children first sometimes. But, if you have to leave, then go ahead," I said quietly, defeated by his words. The pain radiating through my stomach was a stark reminder that I had been overreacting lately. This baby was active, sensitive to every emotion that passed through my body. I knew it was time for me to calm down, for the sake of my baby. Time to suppress my feelings… again.

My expectations of marriage and motherhood were blaringly different from the disturbing reality. Karl's recent subtle shift had put my gut on notice something wasn't quite right, but second-guessing myself kept the battle between intuition and nagging self-doubt going. The twin girls had given me a crash-course of selflessness I wasn't ready for. Always thinking about others and never leaving room for myself was my life's theme. All of this was just too much. Pain hit me again. I grabbed my stomach, hoping the pressure would give me some relief. Then the next one hit like a bolt of lightning, bringing me to my knees. *Don't be a drama queen,* I told myself. My attempt to suppress my scream derived into an agonizing whimper. Karl ran to my side, trying to pull me up. I snatched my arm away.

"I'm okay," I managed to say through gritted teeth, tears falling. My baby wasn't due for another three weeks.

"Lee, oh my God, I'm sorry. I upset you." His voice trembled.

"Just go, I know you're busy." I continued to push him away.

"No, we're going to the hospital." Karl insisted and my world turned upside down.

CHAPTER 1

Baby Blues

looked over at the empty basinet beside my hospital bed. Kaiden's birth had been long and traumatic, totaling twenty hours and resulting in a hysterectomy after delivery. I was beyond devastated that Karl and I were forced to call this a completion to our family. There would be no talks of any more children, that decision was finalized with the birth of Kaiden Michaels. It was settled—twin girls and a boy. But at least I was alive. I had coded because of the enormous loss of blood, and Dr. Young had to make some quick decisions. Karl, of course, was agreeable to whatever would save my life. I imagined he was traumatized as well.

I looked out the window wishing to see a little white bird, a feather or something; anything to symbolize that my best friend, Johnathon, was watching over me. There was nothing, no sign of him, which added more to my devastation. It had been four years since he had passed but I still longed for him, especially during difficult times. This time

I had to be strong and love on this beautiful boy who just changed my life.

Karl walked in the room carrying a bag of snacks I had requested. "Here you go, sweetheart." He was being so loving.

"Thank you." I set the bag beside me on the bed. Karl leaned in and gave me a kiss on the forehead. "Where's my baby?"

"The nurse took him for a while. You need to rest; your body has been through a lot."

"I don't need to rest; I want my baby. I don't trust him out of my sight. Karl, you know that; I told you the same thing after I had the girls."

"I know, I'm sorry," he said. Just as he started to walk out, the nurse came in pushing a little bassinet with Kaiden laying there all swaddled up. He was supposed to be a Jr., but Karl and I had decided to name him Kaiden because we thought he should have his own identity. That name had been used for generations and Karl wanted to break that tradition.

"Here is your baby," she sang. "He is so cute; we can't get enough of him in the nursery."

"Thank you, please hand him to me," I insisted.

"Here you go." She carefully placed Kaiden into my arms and walked out. He slowly opened his eyes, revealing the jade-colored jewels. I took his hat off to examine his head full of light brown curls. He had Karl's face. I reclined my bed slightly and brought him closer to my body. Karl sat at the corner of the bed.

"He's perfect. I love you both so much." He was getting teary eyed. I could tell he was still shaken up about Kaiden's birth.

"I love you, too, and I'm sorry about all of this."

"Sorry about what?"

"I'm sorry I couldn't get through the delivery without all the problems; now I can't have any more children. That's not what we planned."

"None of this is your fault, I'm just happy you are alive. We don't need any more children," he said.

"I know, but I would've liked to have more control over how things went. Anyway, I'm glad Kaiden is here and I'm here, too." I reflected on the whole ordeal. Despite arriving to the hospital in excruciating pain, with obvious signs that something was terribly wrong, they still tried to send me home, saying the baby's heartbeat was fine and the contractions were irregular. Dr. Young showed up and insisted I be admitted. Just as I was getting to the room my water broke, and regular contractions started. After an epidural and several hours of labor, Kaiden arrived. Dr. Young had to stop the delivery and cut the cord, which was wrapped around Kaiden's neck. I thank God that he was born healthy. Soon after, the nurse called Dr. Young back in because my bleeding would not stop and my blood pressure was slowly dropping. Next thing I knew, I was waking up to Karl and my mother standing over me. They looked like they had been crying, so I immediately started screaming for my baby. I thought something had happened to Kaiden, but he was okay. It was me that had crashed and required several rounds of CPR. The hysterectomy was necessary to save my life. I was sad that the birth of our only son, our last child, had to be so traumatic.

"Hello, sunshine," my mom said as she walked into the room.

"Hey, Mom!" I was happy to see her and show off Kaiden again.

"Hey, baby girl. I brought you all the stuff you requested." She set down the overnight bag I had procrastinated about packing for the hospital stay.

"Thank you."

"Kaiden is so cute, he gave us a scare getting here, didn't he?" She reached over to take him out my arms.

"Yes, he did." I smiled.

"I'm so proud of you, Lee. You are so strong getting through all of this."

"Well, I had to. I have my babies to take care of. By the way, where are the girls?" I asked, surprised my mom didn't bring them.

"Oh, they were tired. Rachel wore them out playing in the pool. She's watching them for us now."

"Rachel, isn't that Ronald's daughter? I've only met her a few times and never discussed her watching the girls." I peered at Karl.

"Yes, well, she is taking a break from college and needed a little job. She's so good with the girls, I thought it would be a perfect time for her to help us out," Karl explained.

"So good with the girls… I've never even seen her around them, and like I said before, I wasn't asked about Rachel watching my children." My sharp tone disturbed Karl and alerted my mom I wasn't happy about this. Mom particularly always commented about letting women in your home, around your husband; that is something we didn't do, so I thought.

"Listen, you are in the hospital and even when you get home, we are going to need help, and she is doing fine," Karl advocated for her.

"My mom is here to help; I don't know Rachel," I insisted.

"Yea, but we have a new baby, you just had major surgery, and the girls are a handful; your mother will need help, too."

"I don't know her—period." I glared at Karl.

"Please, Leesha, I'm thinking about you and your needs, that's all. We can talk about it more later, but I don't want you upset." He squeezed my hand, pleading for me to let it go.

I moved and a sharp pain hit me, radiating from my stomach through my butt, down to my thighs. I grimaced and Mom put Kaiden down to help me adjust in bed. She fluffed the pillow behind my back and rubbed my head.

"I'm here for whatever you need, but consider what your husband is saying," she spoke softly, trying to keep me calm.

"Mom please, this is pissin' me off, just stop." Now the pain was bringing tears to my eyes. I pushed the call light for medication. "I'm going to take some pain pills and get some rest. Both of you, please go home and see after my girls. I'm okay with Kaiden."

"I'll go take care of Lizzie and Frankie, you go get something to eat and stay with Lee. It doesn't matter how difficult she's being, she needs someone here," my mom said. I rolled my eyes. "Lee, I know you're feeling crazy with your hormones and everything that has happened, but let Karl be here for you."

"Okay, Mom." I was short. She kissed me and Kaiden then left.

"I'm going to the cafeteria to get a bite. Do you want anything?" Karl asked.

"What is this deal with Ronald's daughter watching Lizzie and Frankie? Me and you have NEVER discussed that. How old is that girl anyway?" I was obviously still upset.

"Ronald has worked for me a long time; he is my lead contractor. So, when he asked if Rachel could help out anywhere for some extra money, I thought this was a great idea. I don't know how old she is… twenty somethin' I guess. She's old enough to watch the girls, so what difference does it make? I'm sorry if you're upset, that wasn't my intention, Lee." His voice softened and he kissed my cheek.

"Okay, but I'd rather my mom watch them. I'll leave it alone and see how things are going when I get home. Thank you for trying to make things easy on Mom and me. I do appreciate you." I gave him a hug, which satisfied him. I figured there was no use in us fighting after all we had been through.

Kaiden let out a little whimper and my breasts ached. It was time to feed him. I wasn't successful in breastfeeding the girls, but I wanted to try again with Kaiden. I had decided to not be too hard on myself about it, but really hoped things went well.

"Karl, can you hand me Kaiden? I'm going to feed him." I asked.

"Yes, I'll stay till he's done, just in case." He gave me a reassuring smile.

"Thanks." I was grateful Kaiden latched on right away. Karl stayed and munched on some of the snacks he had brought.

After Kaiden finished and I changed his diaper, Karl ordered us some steaks and sides from Flemings Steakhouse. The nurse helped me shower after dinner, then Karl and I got comfortable for the night. Luckily, I had a suite on the top floor of the hospital. It was a large room with an extra bed, couch, and huge bathroom. Two nurses staffed my room, so I never had to wait for anything.

After a few days, I was discharged from the hospital. My stay was longer than necessary, but Karl insisted I stayed to make sure everything was good. As soon as I walked through the door, Lizzie and Frankie ran and attached themselves to my leg. They were in their bathing suits and hair was dripping wet. My mom was in the kitchen cooking and wasn't wearing a bathing suit. I hugged the girls and looked out the back door at the patio. Rachel was in a neon green bikini, walking around the pool picking up floaties and towels. My face twisted and I looked back at Mom. She knew I was not happy.

"I've been cooking you a good dinner and thank God Rachel was here to keep the girls occupied." She had a nervous smile. As soon as she finished talking, Rachel came in.

"Hi, Mrs. Michaels. I'm so glad you're home. The girls missed you so much, congratulations on your new baby." Her perfect smile was outlined with nude glossy lips. Her thick, dark brown hair highlighted her clear blue eyes, and her body was reminiscent of the type of women Karl had pictures with on his socials before we dated—super thin.

"Hi, Rachel, thank you for helping with Lizzie and Frankie while I was in the hospital. I'm glad to be home and look forward to things getting back to normal." I wanted to tell her she was no longer needed, but I knew that would cause conflict with me and Karl. I still wanted to know how helpful she was and if she really was harmless.

"Of course, you've been through so much," she commented as she threw on a long cover-up and looked at Mom.

"Lucie, do you want me to do anything else? I can stay and get the girls together."

"No, Rachel, thank you so much. You can head home." Mom couldn't get her out fast enough.

"Okay. Bye, Mrs. Michaels and Lucie. See you later, Karl. Girls give me a hug, I'm leaving," Rachel said as if she had been running my damn house. The girls didn't respond; they were too busy climbing all over Karl and looking at their baby brother. She smiled and left.

"Lucie… you on a first name basis with Ms. Rachel?" Mom rolled her eyes at my sarcastic tone. "I'm just saying; and look at the girls' hair!" Lizzie's wavy hair normally hung loosely down her back was tangled in scattered knots, and Frankie's hair was typically curled in perfect tight coils was now matted. I was pissed. "They need to be bathed, and hair washed and dried. I really don't want them in the pool anymore, the weather is getting ready to change and they're only two. I can't be trynna take care of them if they get sick," I said.

"Yes, ma'am!" Mom's sarcasm matched mine. "Lizzie and Frankie, let's go get bathed and those heads washed." She grabbed the girls off of Karl.

"Thank you, Mom," I said and turned my attention toward Karl. He was holding Kaiden, looking so in love. I didn't want my first night back to be drama filled, so I decided to leave it alone.

"He's beautiful, isn't he," Karl said.

"Yes, I think he's gonna look mostly like you with those green eyes and brown hair." I ran my fingers through Karl's hair. He looked up and leaned in for a kiss.

"Thank you for making me the happiest man alive. I love you and our kids so much." He didn't know how much I needed to hear those words. The fact I couldn't have any more kids had been haunting me and the doubts of Karl's happiness was overwhelming. I felt like my womanhood had been ripped away with no say so. Secretly, my emotions had been all over the place; crying in the shower, trying to sleep but unable to, and faking a smile and excitement when Kaiden was placed in my arms. Don't get me wrong, I loved my baby, but the urge to lay there and wallow in self-pity was stronger sometimes.

The next two weeks were filled with breastfeeding, sleepless nights, and pain. I had opted to only use Tylenol for Kaiden's sake. Lizzie and Frankie still required much of my attention, and I wanted to make them feel just as special as their baby brother. Mom had just gone back to Louisiana but promised to be back in a few months. She had prepped my freezer with homemade meals that were easy to prepare. The housekeeper came in every day to maintain things and the pool was locked up and covered. Karl had gone back to work, and I just had to worry about myself and the kids.

I was still tired, and the girls were in the middle of potty training, which wore me down too.

Karl finally convinced me to let Rachel come back to help with the girls during the day. Even though I put up a fight, I was secretly grateful to have the help. She showed up Monday morning all smiles. She had to bribe the girls with chocolate milk and cartoons to get them out of my room. I was finally able to sleep while Kaiden slept and it felt good to finally catch up on my rest. All I did was put some beef stew in the crockpot, baked some cornbread, lay in bed, and care for the baby. Rachel entertained and fed the girls. When they napped, she came and checked on me, bringing me lunch and whatever else I needed. I didn't know how much Karl was paying her, but at that time I didn't care.

As time went by, I was tearful and on edge about everything. My head and body were achy, and I felt tired all the time. Breastfeeding and caring for Kaiden exhausted me and I had no patience for Karl or the girls. Things got worse when Kaiden had his two-month check-up, and the pediatrician informed me that he was losing weight. All I heard was I failed as a mother again, and I couldn't even successfully feed my baby. It was suggested I supplement with formula. I cried all the way home and Karl tried to console me, suggesting I needed a break from breastfeeding and now I could let other people help feed him. All I heard was now Rachel could feed my baby… in my mind she was taking over my kids, my home, and soon my life.

I had to get her out, so I called my mom to come back to help me. This time, I insisted she bring James, so she could stay longer. Mom heard the desperation in my voice and knew there was something wrong with me.

"Lee, whatever is going on, you need to calm down. You're acting like the world is ending," Mom said.

"Mom, please can you and James come, I need you. Kaiden is losing weight, I can't feed him good, I have no energy, and this girl is taking my life." I knew I was overreacting, but everything felt like an emergency.

"Okay, let me make sure our business is taken care of down here, talk to James, and we will be there. I promise." She was saying anything to calm me down.

"Thank you. When do you think you'll be ready to come so I can get your tickets?" I asked.

"Leesha, I said let me take care of some things and I will let you know." She was irritated with me, so I let it go.

I was still unable to get a grip on my emotions when Karl got home from work that evening. He was at a loss and couldn't figure out why I cried about everything. He finally left the room, allowing me to gather myself. I heard him on the phone and my mind began racing, wondering who he was talking to and why he had to leave the room to do it. I was clearly spiraling and couldn't stop it. Now angry, I stormed into the living room where he was.

"Who is that? Who are you talking to, huh?" I yelled. Karl looked at me, shocked at the crazy lady standing in front of him. I walked toward him and pried the phone out his hand.

"Hello, who's this?" I demanded.

"Leesha, it's Mom." My mom's voice mirrored the shock in Karl's face. "James and I will be there as soon as possible. We are trying to get a flight out now, but I need you to hold on and get yourself together, okay." Her voice was even and controlled.

"Oh, I'm sorry, Mom, I didn't know it was you." I was horrified and embarrassed.

"It's okay, Lee, but I need you to calm down and hold on until I get there," she repeated.

It was clear I was heading into a breakdown, but I refused to completely give that feeling anymore momentum. "Yes, Mom, I'm okay. I'm sorry, I just need some rest." I gave the phone back to Karl and he ended their conversation. He hung up the phone and stared at me. I knew he wanted to go off on me, but instead he decided to be cool.

"Who did you think I was talking to?" he asked.

"I don't know, I'm so sorry." Tears flooded my eyes once again. Karl pulled me into an embrace in a final attempt to comfort me. I felt so foolish.

CHAPTER 2

After Effects

Mom sat on the side of the bed holding my hand as I cried still not knowing why. She had been on duty with Kaiden and keeping me sane for over a week and now she was suggesting something I did not want to consider.

"Leesha, you're crying all the time, and everyone is worried about you."

"I am just tired and seems like I'm not cut out to be a mother, much less a wife to Karl. Not to mention I need that girl out of my house."

"You are a good mother and wife, stop beating yourself up over nothing; that girl is a big help right now and your husband is paying her good money to be here for you and the kids."

"I don't want her touching Kaiden, feeding him, bonding with him. He is my baby."

"We all understand that, and we all see how irrational you're becoming. You've been through a lot with the delivery and surgery, but it's time to turn the page on all that. You have a beautiful life and family. You need to get yourself together and participate in this life of yours." Mom was stern. "Now get up, take a shower, wash that stinky ass hair, and call your doctor for an appointment. You are depressed and need some medication."

"Mom! Really, I express my feelings to you and now I need meds?"

"Leesha, there is no shame in that, so don't get offended. Poor Karl is afraid to say anything to you and the girls miss you. Please, call the doctor."

"No! I'm not crazy and weak. I don't need any damn meds! Now stop it." The conversation was over. I laid back down and tearfully drifted to sleep. It wasn't long before I started to dream.

I was walking in a beautiful garden filled with colorful flowers and butterflies. Johnathon was walking beside me, holding my hand.

"How is it here in heaven?" I asked.

"It's so perfect here, Lee. Had I known this was waiting for me, I would have gotten here sooner. But I did what I was there to do and got here as fast as possible. This is home, you know."

"Yea, it does feel like home," I admitted. "What do you do all day?"

"Well, everyone just spends the day getting ready for our big celebration we have every night. We all have our jobs and I'm the bread baker." He smiled.

"What? You're kidding me." I laughed. Next thing I knew, we were sitting in a little house in front of a wood-burning stove and Johnathon was baking a variety of bread. It smelled amazing.

"You know, Leesha, if you don't like it there, you can just come to heaven and be with me," he said.

"What? Johnathon, but you're dead and here."

"I'm not dead, you are. All you do is lay around and be sad. You don't have to be like that. Come with me."

"I can't. I have my children to live for, they need me. Karl needs me and my mom would be devastated if I left," I said.

"Right, but you're still not happy and let's face it, you would be happy with me, and you know it," he continued.

"No, no… I'm not done. I have to stay, for my babies," I pleaded.

"Okay, then act like it, get up and live, until we meet again," he said before fading away.

I woke up with my heart pounding and chest aching. I didn't tell him I loved him, and I missed him. I should have hugged him, but it was obvious that dream was a message. My mom came in the room as if she had sensed my despair.

"Okay, I'll call and get some help," I said sitting up, still dazed.

"Good." She gave me a smile and walked out.

Subconsciously, I was desperate for help. Johnathon coming to me was comforting but his message was scary. I had been on anxiety and depression medication before and thought I wouldn't need it with this seemingly perfect life. When I got pregnant with the girls, I stopped taking them and was okay until now. I did what my mom said—cleaned myself up and made an appointment.

It took a few weeks for the medication to kick in. Meanwhile, I did my best to fake happiness and control the irritability and sadness that had taken hold of me. Karl stopped walking on eggshells, the girls were all over me again, and Kaiden was solely bottle fed now. That decision took a big weight off of me. Rachel was staying later and later. She and Karl would sit and talk when he got home from work. Mom would usually be in the kitchen preparing dinner, so she didn't really notice. I like to think I had more clarity about the whole Rachel invasion, especially now that I was on medication. But something still didn't sit right. He talked to her at least half an hour before he would even find me to say hi. I started making it a point to sit in the living room when he got home, so I could join their conversation. Rachel would leave in a hurry when I was there. I wanted her out of my house.

"Karl, I need to talk to you," I said to him as he walked out of the bathroom, drying his hair.

"Yea, baby, what's up?"

"I think I'm fine and got a good routine with the kids. I don't need Rachel here anymore."

He froze then turned to me. "You have a good routine because she's here. Are you even thinking about what you're saying?" That comment pissed me off. He had been treating me like I was a child or just crazy.

"I know what I'm saying. Are you even thinking about how you've been talking to me lately? I'm your wife, your children's mother and you're acting like I'm just some annoying woman you're putting up with. If you're tired or don't want me, just say it because you already know..."

"Don't start that, Lee. I'm sorry if I've been coming off as mean or offensive to you, but things are hard for me, too. We're building a whole damn subdivision and everything that could go wrong, is." He laid in the bed next to me and scooped me in his arms. "I never want to hear you say I don't want you because you know you're the love of my life. I miss you, baby." He squeezed me. It felt good to be in his arms again, but I wasn't deterred from my original goal, so back to Ms. Rachel.

"Karl, I don't need nor want her here anymore. Please, things just don't feel right," I pleaded.

"What do you mean 'don't feel right?' Things are okay, we are finally getting into the swing of things and Rachel is a big part of that. Besides, I promised Ronald that she can work with us until she decided about whether she's going back to college or not."

"Well, her decision could take forever, and I think what I want is more important… or it should be." I peered at him, and he avoided looking my way.

"You are more important than her and her stupid decision, but I think we are the ones benefiting from her presence, not the other way around."

"Okay, fine." I gave in, but I'd only conceded to the conversation. I had decided to take matters into my own hands.

One evening, Rachel was hanging around waiting for Karl to get home. I was in the kitchen helping Mom make plates for the girls. I had decided to make Karl's plate and put it in the microwave. I put spaghetti on the plate and turned around to grab a piece of garlic toast for him. When I looked back, Rachel was sprinkling cheese on his spaghetti.

"Oh, I let him do his own cheese if he wants it, and he usually doesn't," I said.

"Well, he likes cheese; I'm sure of it," she countered. My mom stopped and looked at us. She knew this wasn't going to end well for Rachel.

"Put the cheese down, please. I will make my husband's plate, and you are overstepping now."

"I'm just saying, he likes cheese. Maybe his taste has changed since you last made food for him, it's been a while." Her voice was eerily wicked this time.

I stood in her face, close enough to make her feel uncomfortable. "I am his wife, that hasn't changed… I know what he likes. Like I said before, you have overstepped, and your assistance is no longer needed, please do not come back here. Thank you and goodbye." Just as I got those words out, Karl appeared. Rachel turned to him with a complete change in her demeanor. She was back to the cheerful, overly nice young lady.

"Well, Karl, I mean Mr. Michaels, your wife just told me not to come back anymore," she said. Karl tilted his head and stared at me through narrowed eyes.

"What's going on? Lee, I thought we discussed this," he said.

"I have made the decision that she goes, and I will not explain myself." My icy stare notified him I was not to be challenged.

"Okay, I will talk to you later, Rachel. Thank you for all the help you have given us these last few months," Karl said.

"You're very welcome, Karl. Bye Lucie and James." They did not respond. She went over and gave the girls a kiss, which they ignored, distracted by their bowls of cheesy spaghetti.

"Bye, Mrs. Michaels." She acknowledged me to keep up the show for Karl.

"Goodbye." I gave a wave as she walked out the door.

"What the hell happened? Lee, I thought we talked about this?" Karl asked, surprisingly calm.

"She made the right decision. I think Rachel was getting a little too comfortable, and she was disrespectful to Leesha just now," my mom interjected.

"It was time for her to leave, Karl. Go get comfortable, I have your plate ready," I said. He walked away. Mom turned toward me.

"Can you believe that heffa? She really tried you." Mom shook her head in amazement.

"I know, something about her never felt right to me," I admitted.

Dinner was uneventful and Karl seemed normal, not upset or anything. I gave the girls a bath and read them a story before they went to bed. Mom and James took over Kaiden for the night; he had a crib in their room too. That would give Karl and me some time alone.

It had been almost four months since the delivery and hysterectomy, and I had been cleared for sex at two months. Karl had not attempted to touch me, but I didn't blame him. Things had been rocky, and it was obvious I wasn't in the mood. My desire for Karl had been growing stronger. I came to bed with a black lace tank top and matching boy shorts. My body wasn't how I wanted it. I was clearly out of shape but wasn't disgusting. Mom had brought my attention to my lack of concern for my weight a month ago, so I had been cutting back, taking walks around the neighborhood, and doing squats in the bathroom before my showers. I wasn't obsessing about my weight, but I was concerned.

I slid in bed and slipped my hand around Karl; he shifted but didn't turn toward me. I snuggled into him, which was usually his hint. Once again, no response.

"Karl, are you mad at me?" I asked.

"No. What could I possibly be mad at you for?" There was a hint of sarcasm in his voice.

"Rachel, for one," I said bluntly.

"We talked about it, and you did what you wanted to do," he complained.

"She was here for me, not you. I know you and her may have confused that, but let's get it straight now. She was here to help me, not be your evening eye candy and play your young wifey while I was laid up trying to recover from having our child, getting my uterus snatched out and dying. Sorry I wasn't myself. But I'm back, and to her dismay, I survived. She is no longer needed, I want my house back, my kids, my husband."

"Eye candy, young wifey? You sound ridiculous." He shook loose from me and scooted to the edge of the bed like he wanted to be as far away from me as possible. I turned away, letting sadness overcome me once again.

CHAPTER 3

The New Normal

Mom and James stayed for two more weeks, and I was getting used to my new routine. I hired a personal trainer to come to my home. I had decided to forget about Karl's sour attitude and focus on myself. Once he saw I couldn't give two shits about him or Rachel, he started coming around. We were at least able to have cordial conversation. Kaiden was becoming the cutest, chubbiest baby ever and the girls always wanted to help with him.

The subdivision that the company had been working on was complete and there was going to be a party with all the stakeholders of this project. I really didn't want to go but had to. It was a formal event, which was a great time to finally put myself all the way together and maybe Karl would see what he had been missing. Mrs. Ruiz, the previous nanny we had for the girls, was scheduled to watch the kids. She was my real go-to but had stopped her nanny business to take care of her grandchildren.

I decided to show off my beautiful caramel skin with a simple, black spaghetti strapped dress and black, Red Bottom stilettos. My hair was straightened and parted down the middle and make-up was simple but stunning, thanks to my regular glam squad who came to the house when I had to go to events.

The party was being held at a huge house out in the country. We drove down a path illuminated by lights carefully strung in the trees. Our car had a mini bar, and I had two drinks by the time our driver opened the door. Karl had stared at me the whole time and he did not drink. I wanted something to take the edge off, and hopefully loosen my nerves so I could socialize with ease. Karl didn't tell me I looked pretty or anything. But I knew I looked good and was craving attention.

I recognized a few of Karl's workers and associates when we arrived. People were walking around, having their fake conversations, and laughing. There were tables setup in the back and several stations with different foods. I decided to get something on my stomach to offset the alcohol I had consumed on the way in. A server was placing some sliced turkey on my plate when Ronald, Rachel's father, stood next to me.

"Hi, Mrs. Michaels, how are you this evening?"

"I'm fine, how are you?"

"I'm doing well. I just wanted to come over and thank you," he said.

"Thank me for what?"

"The opportunity you and Mr. Michael's gave Rachel."

"Oh well, we appreciate her help," I said, hoping to cut the conversation short.

"She loved helping with your children, but she really loves working in the office with Mr. Michaels. She's learning so much," he continued.

"Really, I'm glad. What is it that she does again?" I was stunned by his revealing comment.

"I think she answers phones, plans business trips, file stuff. I don't know but she stays busy. Hopefully she moves back home and goes to college and finishes her masters."

"Oh, she doesn't live at home anymore?"

"No, she moved out a few months ago, I guess she's getting paid well."

"Wow, congratulations to her. Does she have a room-mate at least? Apartments are so expensive now-a-days." I kept digging for information.

"No, she's solo. Hey, I gotta run, my wife is calling me. Rachel is here, hopefully she gets a chance to say hi."

"Yes, for sure. See you later, Ronald, it was nice chatting with you." My heart was beating out of my chest. I wanted to punch Karl in the face. Why was he hiding this from me. I sat down and my appetite was suddenly gone. I was scat-tering food around my plate when Karl came to the table, and I immediately confronted him.

"Karl, I saw Ron and he thanked you for giving Rachel a job in your office. Really, when were you gonna tell me you hired her to work there?" I asked.

"I didn't think I had to check with you to hire someone," he shot back.

"Not just someone, but Rachel, the woman that I don't like or want around my children and definitely not my husband."

"Here we go; must we have this conversation now?"

"Well, I just now found out. We could've had this conversation before you even hired her," I said with a tight-lipped smile.

"Look, I don't have to check with you to make decisions about my family's company. Besides, there's nothing you need to worry about; Rachel is just an employee, I just talked to her at the house because she was helping you and the kids. I had to be friendly. Was I supposed to be rude?" He let out an exasperated sigh.

"Your family's company? What am I? Aren't I family, too? Doesn't my opinion matter? That bitch is a snake in the grass, and I'll say it once again, I prefer her to be far away from my husband, with her flirtatious ass." I threw my fork down, attracting the attention of a couple sitting at the next table.

"Stop it, you're being ridiculous. I'm asking you to trust me and let this shit go. I have hired her and that's it, get over it." His clinched jaw and gritted teeth was my sign that the conversation was over.

"Fine, I guess I have no choice but to get over it. It's okay, I don't have feelings anyway."

"Lee, I'm sorry, just don't be mad. Let's have a good night, please." Karl was trying to soften the conversation to avoid more embarrassment.

"I said it's fine. Yea, let's have a good night." I gave in with the intent on taking care of this Rachel problem later.

"Hey, I see Mr. Jameson by the bar, I need to talk to him and try to secure another contract. I'll be back." He gave me a kiss on the cheek and headed toward the bar. I decided to leave the table and take a walk, too.

I made my way down an empty hall in search of a restroom or maybe somewhere private to stew in anger. I heard some footsteps rushing behind me and turned to see Mike.

"Hey, I just wanted to say congratulations on the new baby." He smiled.

"Thank you." My stomach tightened. Karl still didn't know Mike and I knew each other, much less used to sleep together. I couldn't even say we dated. Looking back, it was purely sexual. What were the odds Mike would become Karl's company lawyer?

"You look great, Lee." He rubbed my arm.

"Thanks, so do you. Are you here alone?" I looked to see if anyone was coming behind him.

"Yes, my fiancé couldn't make it." Mike and his wife had divorced and now he was preparing to marry someone else. Poor lady was all I thought.

"Where's Karl?" he asked.

"Who cares where he is," I commented before thinking. Mike raised his eyebrow.

"Is everything okay?" he inquired.

"Umm, yeah, just saying he's probably running around chit chattin' with everyone. Events like these make me tired."

"Me too. I'd rather be at home, listening to music, drinking Crown, and having some great conversation." He gazed at me.

"Oh, that all sounds familiar but dangerous." I cursed myself for having the fleeting thought that those were actually good times we spent together, when they were nothing but toxic. My anger at Karl urged me to flirt back.

"Dangerous! Dangerous how?" Mike knew he had baited me in. What he didn't know was it was by my choice, not by what he considered charming or slick conversation.

"Well, for one, we were always chilling at my house because you had a whole wife at home, sir," I teased.

"Yup. Can you believe I'm actually getting married again? And now, you're married with kids. Damn, that's crazy." He shook his head.

"Wow, that is crazy," I agreed.

"But you're still sexy as fuck; I'll give that to you." His eyes traveled up my body briefly stopping at my breasts, then back up to my face.

"Okay, I better go." I started backing away, but really wanted to stay because it had been months since I had heard a kind word or felt the touch of my husband. Deep down, I welcomed the attention. Mike picked up on my pretending to want to escape from him. He still had the gift of reading my eyes and body language… reading me. Flashbacks of us fucking caught me by surprise, but I didn't react to the vivid thoughts in my head. He grabbed my arm and stepped closer.

"Remember our last night together? That night I decided to really let you go after you ghosted me." His face was tense.

"I don't want to talk about us or the past." I shuddered under the weight of his hand.

"That was the hardest shit I ever had to do—telling you I would leave you alone so you could move on. That shit right there, ripped my fucking heart out." He gave a nervous laugh and dropped my arm. "Now I'm working for your husband. Ain't that a bitch?"

"Yea, small world…" I replied. "Listen, let's not make things awkward, okay." My heart twisted in my chest. *Where is that narcissistic bastard? Who is this man in front of me drawing me in?*

"It's not my intention to make things weird. But I'll probably never have this chance again. So, I took it. Forgive me, Mrs. Michaels." He walked away, leaving me longing for another touch or maybe even a secret kiss. I rubbed my arms to control the goosebumps Mike had caused with his presence. I was in deep shit because a large part of me desired to go after him. I rationalized it by thinking about the Rachel situation and the lack of affection from Karl.

Just as I turned to walk back down the hall, I heard a door open, and Rachel appeared. She looked at me and a silly smirk crossed her face. I wondered if she heard Mike and me talking. But, at this point, I really didn't fucking care. I opted not to speak to her and made my way back to the party.

I found Karl standing at the bar, chatting with an older man and who I assumed his wife. I walked up and slipped my hand into Karl's. He looked at me and surprisingly there was a genuine smile. He let go of my hand and put his arm around my waist, drawing me closer. After the couple left, he gave me a kiss on the cheek.

"You look stunning tonight, Lee."

"Thank you." I still wanted to investigate this Rachel deal more, but the urgency had decreased because hell... I had secrets, too. If Karl wanted to play that game, well he had no idea who his opponent was. I knew I couldn't be the one to fuck our lives up, but payback dick, locked up in an unbreakable case wasn't a bad idea—at least I could fantasize.

Surprisingly, I didn't run into Mike or Rachel again that night. I didn't know what had gotten into Karl, but he couldn't keep his hands off me when we got home. I did welcome the long-awaited attention. When we made it home, I got into the shower and I was almost done when the shower door opened, letting a cool draft of air in. I glanced over my shoulder to see Karl standing there. His body just as beautiful as the day we first met—muscular, smooth, and perfect. I crossed my arms over my body, covering the remnants of pregnancy, childbirth, and surgery. He gently pulled my arms down, exposing me. I dropped my head, ashamed I hadn't started working out sooner and comparing myself to my nemesis that now worked in the office with Karl. He lifted my head and kissed me; all the doubts and insecurities faded away. My body had been waiting for Karl's touch and from the way he was kissing me, he had been longing for me, too. His tongue glided down to my breasts, there was a slight ache, but I encouraged the attention. His tongue swirled around each nipple, but he was careful not to be too aggressive. He slowly slid to his knees, licking and kissing my body along the way. I shivered when he made it to my pussy. He lifted my leg, placing it over his shoulder and I moaned as he gently licked my center. I allowed him to please me, guiding my body to ecstasy. When he was done, I shivered from the orgasm he had easily brought out of me. He led me to bed and we both anxiously got reacquainted with each other, kissing and caressing, both satisfying the desire we had been holding in for so long. He slowly entered me, and I instantly relaxed allowing him to glide in easily. He gasped in relief of finally feeling the warmth of my pussy, giving me encouragement to roll my hips meeting the cadence of his eager strokes. He pulled out in an effort to regain control then entered me again, lifting my leg and securing it around his waist. His dick massaged my pussy until we both finally came.

❀ ❀ ❀

We woke up to the sound of thunder and Lizzie's scream. She was always afraid of rain, thunder, and lightning. Next, it was Frankie yelling, "Mommy!" I knew it. Lizzie was the dramatic one and Frankie was the tough one, so Lizzie stayed on Frankie's nerves. I got up and pulled Kaiden's crib away from the window, hoping he did not wake up too, and headed to the girls' room. By the time I got there, Lizzie was in a full-blown meltdown and Frankie was sitting in Lizzie's bed, forcing a teddy bear into her arms. I scooped them up and carried them to our bed. When I got back in the room, Karl was sitting up with the lamp on, waiting for the inevitable sleepover. Kaiden remained asleep. Lizzie stayed glued to me and Frankie happily went to Karl's side of the bed. It was just past 1 a.m., so it was going to be rough for the next few hours since both girls were wild sleepers.

When they both went to sleep, Karl looked at me and mouthed, "I love you, Lee."

"I love you, too," I whispered back. I felt so happy and content at that moment. *How can I let Mike get into my head for a single second? How can I doubt Karl's loyalty? But why the secrets about Rachel?* I decided on doing a little investigation of my own about that.

We were all awake by 9 a.m. and Karl was in the restroom. I was holding Kaiden, and the girls were beside me. I grabbed my phone and took a picture of us cuddled

32

together. I admit, I looked pretty laying there with my babies, so I posted it to my socials. I got a message alert and saw Mike's name.

Damn, that's supposed to be us, you look so beautiful. *Now he's being bold, what the hell is he thinking?* I deleted the message with no response, but admittedly there was an emergence of butterflies in my stomach. *Damn…*

CHAPTER 4

Planning for Disaster

On Monday morning, I got a call from Mrs. Ruiz. She talked about how good the kids had been and how she missed being here. Then she confessed that her daughter had gotten laid off and she would be watching her own children for a while. Mrs. Ruiz asked if she could pick up some hours with us again. I was all too happy to tell her yes. This would be great. I needed time for myself and wanted to get out of the house. Karl was more than agreeable to Mrs. Ruiz coming back. I was sure he thought I forgot about Rachel, but with Mrs. Ruiz back, I would have time to see what was really going on with this made-up position for her.

It took a while to get settled into our new routine, time was racing, and the girls' birthday was coming soon. I had started planning for a big party and sending out invites. My mom and James were coming back and surprisingly my half-sister, Leanna, agreed to come. I felt nervous about Mom and her being in the same room, but Leanna and I had grown closer, and I wanted to maintain that relationship. I stopped at Karl's office to discuss caterers for the party. As soon as I walked in, I saw Rachel prancing around like she owned the place.

"Oh hello, Mrs. Michaels, are you here for Karl. Um I mean Mr. Michaels?" She smiled.

"Yes, of course I'm here to see Karl. How are you liking your position?" I probed.

"I love it here." Her smile annoyed the shit out of me.

"What exactly is it that you do?" I continued.

"I mostly help with contracts and do whatever else needs to be done. I just float around trying to make things easier for Mr. Michaels."

"Great, so you have no real title?"

"Not really but I definitely make life easier for him," she reiterated.

"Right." I was heated. *This bitch just running around being a servant to my husband.*

Karl's office door opened, and he had a weird look on his face when he saw me talking to Rachel. "Lee, come on in, I was waiting for you." I walked in.

"Karl…" I started and he was already rolling his eyes like he didn't want to hear it. "I was trying to figure out what Rachel does here."

"She works here, and you have never asked about anyone else's position, so why are you so fixated on her? What is it with you and her?"

"I just don't like her; I don't trust her," I confessed.

"What about me? Don't you trust me?" he asked.

"Yes, but I'm not comfortable with her. Don't my feelings matter?"

"Of course, you matter more than anything in my life. Rachel is here because she needs a job, and her father worked with us for years. I can at least do him this favor. She also is a good employee."

"Okay, I guess my feelings don't matter, but Ronald's request to keep his daughter employed does," I countered.

"Quit saying that, I already said you do and there is nothing to be worried about." He sat at his desk and started going through some papers, signaling he was done with the conversation. That pissed me off, but I kept my cool.

"Anyway, I got three caterers we need to choose from for the girls' birthday party. We need to decide if we will open up the pool, if so, I want at least two lifeguards. Also, decide on what kind of bouncy house and entertainment. I was considering a clown, face painting, or a magician. I'm hiring someone to be in charge of the games. How many people from the company are coming?"

"Damn, you got a lot going on. At least thirty people have said they were coming, mostly the ones with the kids. What kind of caterers?"

"BBQ, pasta bar, or hamburgers and hotdogs with a variety of sides at each bar," I answered. Then Rachel knocked and walked in without permission.

"Excuse me, but Mr. Michaels, we better go. It's going to take us about thirty minutes to get to the property." She looked at me and smiled.

"Umm, yea right. Lee, can we finish talking about this tonight?" Karl and Rachel stared at me. *Ain't this some shit?*

"If you're too busy and have more important things to do, then I will make the decisions myself; I need to retain these people." I took a deep breath to keep my composure and walked out.

The elevator opened and I stormed out with angry tears in my eyes. How could Karl have such disregard about my feelings. All he had to do was let her go, but he was blind to her flirtatious behavior toward him and her taunting me. Maybe I was being irrational, and the medication wasn't setting right with my mind, but I refused to gaslight my own damn self into thinking I was imagining this shit. Still deep in thought, I bumped into someone, and all the papers flew out of my folder. I looked up to see Mike.

"Lee, what's wrong with you? Are you crying?" he asked when I dropped to the floor to pick up my papers.

"No, I'm just in a hurry." I lied. He helped me gather the last few pamphlets.

"Just slow down. Are you good?"

"Yes, um what are you doing here anyway?" I asked, wiping my face.

"I was supposed to meet with Karl to get these documents signed," he said.

"Really, well he was leaving with Rachel to go to some property… so they said," I scoffed.

"Oh, he must've forgotten." Mike avoided my gaze. I wondered if he knew something but chose not to ask for my sanity.

"Well, he has a lot of other things on his mind, certainly not his daughters' birthday party." I couldn't help but to make a comment.

"No, I don't think that's it, and believe me, Lee, I know what you're trynna say. But I never got that impression."

"Whatever, Mike. Are you coming to the girls' party? Please bring your fiancé," I said, trying to get myself back into character.

"Yes, we're coming."

"Great, I'll see you there." I started walking away, and he grabbed my arm.

"Lee, you wanna go somewhere and talk?"

"No, I don't," I quickly answered.

"Okay." He let me go just in time for the elevators to open and for Karl, Rachel, and another employee to walk out. We all froze and looked at each other. Karl and I locked eyes then he looked at Mike.

"Hey, Karl, I brought the documents to sign for the Regan contract. Everything appears to be in order. Do you want to sign now, or do you want me to come back later?" Mike asked, breaking the awkward silence.

"I'll sign now, I trust you," Karl answered Mike, giving me another glance. I ignored him and walked out.

I waited in my car to watch Karl and Rachel come out. Karl and the other male employee got in the front seat and Rachel got in the back, and they left. I drove away, still upset.

Finally, it was the day of the party. I had been running around crazy getting everything organized. I admit that I over did it for the girls, but this party also doubled as an annual get together for the company's employees and their families. Since the expenses were all on Karl and he didn't have time to help plan, I chose everything. The pool was open with three lifeguards, I chose all three caterers and had them set up in different areas of the yard, and all the entertainment was hired as well. Most of all, I was excited about Leanna being there. She and my mom stayed far away from each other.

Leanna and I were in the pool with the girls who played with false reassurance provided by their brightly colored floaties. Lizzie screamed every time she was splashed, and Frankie purposely kicked her legs extra hard in an obvious effort to upset her sister.

"That's it, we're getting out because you girls are not behaving." I decided to spare me and Leanna from the dramatic Lizzie and Frankie show. Lizzie screamed in opposition and Frankie leaped out and ran away. I knew she was going to Karl. My mother came and got Lizzie to go sit with her and Francine. Leanna and I found an empty table to talk.

"I'm so glad you came down, Leanna. The girls love having you here."

"Thank you for inviting me and I'm glad I accepted the invite this time," she admitted.

"So, catch me up on your life, school, are you dating anyone?" I asked.

"Med school is intense of course; I have PTSD just thinking about it. Dating, no way, absolutely no time for that. I have my friends of course, but that's all."

"Little Leanna, a doctor; I'm so proud of you," I said.

"I'm proud of you, sister. You have a beautiful life after all you been through when we were kids." She squeezed my hand.

"Yes, we both came out good, better than expected," I agreed.

We talked for a while, ignoring all the chaos of the party. Soon, Karl came over toting Frankie. He gave her to me, and I took her in the house to use the restroom and clean her sticky hands. When I came back out, he and Leanna were chatting away. I took that time to slip away and check on Kaiden and Mrs. Ruiz. On the way back out, I spotted Mike and his fiancé. He immediately turned my way, almost like he felt my presence. I headed over and greeted them. His fiancé was the complete opposite of his ex-wife; she was tall and thin with long hair. I pulled my cover-up tighter in a failed attempt to cover my thighs.

"Hello, how are you two doing?" I asked.

"Hey, Lee, we're good. This is a nice party. Looks like the kids are having a ball." Mike's informal greeting caused his fiancé to give him an inquiring look.

"Yes, they are. I wanted to do something nice before they started preschool and this is the company get together too, so I had to do it big."

"I see." Mike's smile still warmed my center. Of course, it didn't take much to get a reaction out of me now-a-days because Karl was holding out again.

"Well, thank you for coming out. Y'all enjoy." I walked away with the familiar feeling of Mike's eyes following me.

I spent some time sitting by the pool talking to Mikayla, Leanna, and some of the other ladies. The bar was not too far away so I found myself overindulging on the drinks. It was late, so most of the people with younger kids had left and now it was mainly adults hanging out. Mom and James had taken the girls in, and Mrs. Ruiz was caring for Kaiden.

Karl and Mike were sitting at a table. I wondered what they were talking about. I decided to take Karl a drink and Mikayla gave me the 'Oh shit, don't start' look. She was the only one that knew about my past with Mike, and she also knew me and alcohol was a disaster waiting to happen.

"Here you go, honey." I handed Karl the drink and bent down, hugging him around his neck.

"Thank you, babe." He could tell by my little slur of words and glossy eyes that I'd had too much to drink. He put his arm around my waist and guided me to the chair next to him, right across from Mike. I crossed my legs toward Karl, giving Mike the full view of my thigh. Mike squirmed in his chair, and I cut my eyes at him with a small side grin that only he could see. Sliding my hand down my thigh, my seduction of Mike continued. I felt a squeeze on my arm to look up to see Mikayla pulling me away.

"Sorry, guys, I'm taking my girl inside with me," she said. Karl looked relieved, but Mike looked like he wanted to follow my ass inside.

"What is it?" I asked Mikayla as I followed her.

"Girl, I had to get you. You're over there showing all your ass to Mike. He looked so uncomfortable, but horny too. Shit, I thought he was gonna drop to his knees and give you head or something," she said, half-drunk herself.

"Eat my pussy, I wish! Mike don't even eat pussy." I laughed loudly. Just as I said that, Mike's fiancé walked around the corner and gave me and Mikayla a strange look. My heart fell to my stomach. She stood there staring long enough to make us completely uncomfortable, then walked away.

"Oh my God," Mikayla and I said in unison.

"You think she heard us?" I asked, acting like I didn't see the look on her face.

"Yea, she definitely heard us."

"Well, she didn't know which Mike we were talking about." I was in denial.

"Really, except your husband's name is Karl." Mikayla rolled her eyes. "Girl, promise you're done for the night. Just go to your room and go to bed. I'm going home, I can't stay and save you from yourself."

"Okay, girl. Imma go wash all this pool water off me and take my ass to bed," I promised.

Karl came to bed about two hours later after he saw all the vendors off and shut down the house.

"You did a great job on the party, Lee. Everyone was really impressed. Thank you for working so hard to get it all together," he said, crawling into bed.

"Thanks, babe." I was glad he was happy but was too tired for the conversation. I felt his hand glide around my waist, pulling me close to him.

"You were a little tipsy tonight."

"Yea, I was just trying to relax after planning this party," I answered. Karl's hand was now caressing my thigh and sliding around between my legs. I turned toward him and gave him the kiss I had been waiting to give him for weeks. Karl was as desperate as I was, and he quickly took my T-shirt off. He slowed himself down and gently kissed my breasts, slowly licking each one; he appreciated their fullness. He came back up and gave me a passionate kiss, then made his way down decorating my body with kisses until reaching my pussy. I felt his nose on my clit as he inhaled and moaned, taking a long slow lick causing me to tremble. I released the moan that had been trapped in me for so long. He slowly devoured my pussy, relishing in my excitement until I came. Karl slid back up, placing my legs over his shoulders and entered me. He gave me a few strokes, stopped, and took some deep breaths to compose himself.

"Oh fuck, oh fuck, I miss that pussy, baby," he groaned, slowly regaining his momentum, blessing me with slow, steady thrusts. Karl's dick was still amazing. I rocked my hips to his rhythm, making him remember how great we were together. He stopped, squeezed my thigh and groaned. "Turn over, so I can fuck that pussy from the back." I complied, and he started stroking me from the back with more urgency.

"Yes, yes…" I gasped feeling the familiar tingle in my belly right before I came. Karl pulled out, taking time to lick my pussy from the back, causing me to quickly cum again. Then he started to fuck me again. He finally came, collapsed on me, and slowly kissed the back of my neck.

CHAPTER 5

Failed Seduction

I decided to surprise Karl at his office. My body was shaping back up nicely, and I felt confident enough to slip on some lingerie. I wore a red lace teddy and red heels under a black trench coat. It was a little breezy outside so I could pull it off.

I got off the elevator and his secretary gave me an inquiring look. I waved at her and kept walking then knocked on Karl's door.

"Come in!" he yelled.

"Good afternoon," I said as I walked in. His eyes shot up.

"Good afternoon. And what did I do to deserve this surprise?" he asked with a wide smile on his face.

"Well, I just thought I'd come by to see my beautiful husband," I said.

"Okay, what's with the coat? Is it getting that cold outside?" he asked.

"No, like I said, I came to see you and… surprise." I gave him what I thought was a seductive smile as I opened the coat revealing the red lace teddy.

"Wow, Oh my God. You look sexy as hell." He was slowly walking toward me.

"Only for you, baby," I said, opening the coat wider.

"Damn, thank you," he moaned, giving me a passionate kiss. He backed away and said, "But I can't do this right now, I have meetings all afternoon."

"You can't spare thirty minutes? I'll make it worth your while." I rubbed his chest as I spoke, lips almost touching his.

"Can we just continue this tonight?" he asked.

"There's nothing to continue, we haven't even started." My hand traveled down to his dick, and I slowly started getting on my knees. He grabbed my arm, pulling me up.

"No, Lee, I said I was busy." He had a tense look on his face and humiliation hit me. Why was he denying me? We had sex in his office before and it was so exciting. Now things were all of a sudden different. I was confused.

"Karl, what is wrong? I'm here, I wanna be with you. Please don't do me like this." I was starting to feel more sadness than anger now. Then there was a knock, and someone tried turning the doorknob. Karl closed my coat and hurried to the door, cracking it open. I heard Rachel's voice.

"Hey, Karl, you ready?" she asked.

"Give me a minute," he said and shut the door. He looked at me. "You got to go, Lee."

"I see." Tears filled my eyes as I buttoned up my coat and walked out. Rachel was standing outside the door. "He's all yours," I said as I passed her.

I sat in my car crying. How could he do me like this? I had to build up a lot of courage to even try this. I was so desperate to get us back on track; I would do practically anything. But I didn't do well with rejection wrapped in humiliation. Karl seemed to care more about plans with Rachel than me. He could have told her to give him some time. But once again, he chose her over me. How much more could I stand. A knock on my window startled me. I looked up to see Mike standing there. I rolled down the window, forgetting I had unbuttoned my coat as soon as I had got into the car. He looked at the completely inappropriate outfit I was wearing.

"Umm..." He covered his mouth, not knowing what to say.

"Oh, sorry. I was trying to surprise Karl," I said, still tearful.

"From the look on your face, things didn't go well," he said, watching me struggle to button up my coat.

"No, he was too busy. He is always too busy for me... him and Rachel again," I commented.

"Oh... calm down, you shouldn't even be behind a wheel this upset."

"Well, where should I be? I'm not welcomed in there." I was feeling more defeated.

"Leesha, do you want to go somewhere and talk?" he asked.

"No, Mike! I'm fucking naked and can't go anywhere."

"Okay, I understand. Why don't you go get dressed and we can meet for a coffee or something. I hate to see you like this." His voice was surprisingly genuine. "Please, just meet me."

I looked in the passenger's seat and there was my gym bag. "I have gym clothes," I said.

"Great. Put them on and follow me." He walked away and got into his SUV. I slid the seat back and reclined it to quickly slip on my sweatpants, t-shirt, and gym shoes. When I was done, I turned on my car signaling to him that I was ready, and we drove away.

Mike and I sat in the coffee shop and updated each other on our lives.

"I can't believe it; Leesha is now a mother of three." Mike smiled as he took a sip of coffee.

"Yes, it's surreal to me, too. But I love those babies and couldn't imagine life without them," I admitted. "Kaiden's delivery was hard, I actually loss so much blood and coded. Long story short, I ended up with a hysterectomy." I blinked back tears, focused on stirring my coffee. Mike grabbed my hand.

"I'm sorry all that happened to you." The warmth of his touch comforted me. I grabbed his other hand, and we sat there for several minutes, just holding hands. I felt like my soul needed that moment.

"Thank you, for being here," I finally said.

"Of course, always for you." Mike always found a way to break down my defenses.

"So, tell me how you met Sasha, the engagement; I want to know everything," I said, trying to act cheerful.

"We actually met at a wedding. She was the wedding coordinator for my friend. So, you can only imagine how she is planning her own wedding. That shit is crazy stressful." He shook his head.

"Well, you knew what the assignment was, hookin' up with a wedding coordinator," I laughed.

"Damn right! Hell, I was tired of being alone anyway. But she is everything a man would want in a wife; beautiful, smart, caring, ride or die type of woman."

"That's good. I'm happy for you."

"Yea, but she ain't no damn Leesha Roberts though." His eyes met mine.

"Don't start, Mike. Ain't nobody like me. You'll never find another," I laughed.

"You right; but you are right here, so why would I go looking?"

"Aren't you happy to be getting married?"

"Yea, I'm very happy. But that don't change the fact that my fuckin' body, my fuckin' mind always craves you," he admitted.

"Same." *I can't believe I just said that! Lee, what in the fuck are you doing?* My mind scolded me. Mike's eyes glimmered.

"Same… is that all you got to say?" He pulled for more.

"I said too much already," I confessed. The muscles in his arms tensed and I couldn't stop staring at him. His chocolate skin and muscular physique still captivated me.

"Leesha, come by my place sometime, please." Mike was not holding back anymore. "We could have a drink and talk; I miss talking to you."

"Is that all you miss, is talking?"

"No, I miss those legs wrapped around me, the softness of your skin, the taste of your lips; I could go on, if you want me to." His stare made me nervous.

"No, I've heard enough. So, you know I can't come to your house, especially after what you said."

"Think about it; I mean no harm and won't do anything you don't want me to do."

"We better go." I stood up and grabbed my purse.

"Right." Mike got up and we left, both going opposite directions but really wanting to go to the same place.

I was getting myself into trouble. But it was nice to have someone to reenforce the fact I was still sexy after Karl's rejection. Honestly, I didn't even feel like I had done anything wrong. After all, it was just coffee between old friends.

CHAPTER 6

Sisterly Bond

After overcoming another bout of depression, I decided to shower and start to actually live life again. I had worn my bed and couch out with vicious cycles of sleeping, crying, and TV marathons. But feeling like today was a new day, I got to moving. I had just turned off the water when I heard my phone ringing. Leanna's name flashed across the screen.

"Hey, Leanna. How are you?" I answered.

"Hello, Lee. I'm great, just calling to check on you."

"I'm doing okay, today's a good day," I updated her. She had been calling me trying to keep my spirits up.

"Good, I've been thinking about you and our last conversation about Karl. I was hoping things were getting better," she said.

"Things are pretty much the same with him, but I'm trying to get myself out of this hole, at least for the kids."

"Is he still coming home late and not being attentive to you?" I had been using her as my sounding board, so she knew everything that was happening.

"Yes," I responded dryly because I really didn't feel like talking about it.

"Do you still think it's that Rachel chick?" she pushed.

"I don't know what else to think. What other explanation could it be? But enough about that, how's school going?" I asked, desperate to change the subject.

"School's okay. So, has he even touched you? I know you miss him."

"No, and frankly I don't want to talk about it."

"Wow, I'm sorry, sister. But he's such a jerk. You deserve so much better," she started in.

"Leanna, I really don't want to go there. I was having a good day. Whatever is going on with Karl, he has to figure that out. He knows what he has here and more importantly I know who I am and my worth, so at this point it's not my problem anymore. I have to start living for the kids and myself." I'd hoped to sound convincing enough to end the conversation about Karl. Honestly, I was too weary to hear all the negative comments about my husband and marriage.

"Well good, I'm glad you're putting yourself first. I agree, whatever outside ass he is getting, doesn't matter. He definitely knows where home is," she said.

"Oh, I gotta go, I hear Kaiden waking up." I lied.

"Okay, sister, love you. We'll talk later."

"Love you too, bye." I hung up the phone and took a slow, deep breath to combat the overwhelming feeling of sadness. When I started confiding in Leanna, she was positive, and I would leave our conversations hopeful and happy. Lately, it was the complete opposite; I felt worse and thought maybe she wanted me to leave Karl and be done with the drama.

After pulling myself together, I went to the kitchen. Mom was standing over the stove stirring a pot of gumbo. The girls were sitting at the table eating rice mixed with chunks of chicken, and cornbread.

"These girls love to eat; they couldn't wait for everything to get done," she said.

"Grandma cook so good!" Lizzie exclaimed.

"Yea, I love Grandma, and her food is so good!" Frankie chimed in.

"Everything smells delicious, Mom. Thank you for doing dinner again."

"No problem, baby. I'm leaving tomorrow so I'm making enough to put in the freezer." Her freezer meals had been saving my life lately. I did appreciate Karl for financing Mom's frequent trips here to help and keep me company.

"I'm sure James misses you," I said.

"I'm sure he doesn't. I know he eats whatever he wants and loving it. I just pray that man don't have another heart attack. Next time, he's coming with me," she said.

"Hopefully you can take a break from here, but I don't mind you and James being here," I admitted.

"Well, we love being here for the girls and Kaiden, those are our babies." She smiled.

"Leanna called." I usually didn't talk about Leanna to Mom, but this particular conversation was weighing heavy on me. Mom didn't really care for me building a relationship with Leanna, but I wasn't sure why. I thought she didn't like the dreadful things from her past being so close to home.

"Really, how did that go?" Her face remained expressionless as she stirred the gumbo.

"She is trying to be there for me in her own way, I guess."

"Listen, Leesha, be careful with her. I know she is your half-sister, but you really didn't grow up with her, and when someone hates your momma, they can't really like you. That's just facts." My mom spoke like she had been waiting to get that out.

"Mom, you did shoot and kill her… I mean our dad." I was not sure why I was so defensive when it came to Leanna.

"Okay, here we go. Yes, I did kill the man that abused my only daughter when I entrusted him to take care of her and also the man that came to my home and brutally attacked me. I don't mean to sound insensitive but now, I'm fighting for you and your mental health. I want to make sure that everyone around you means you good. I have to say what my spirit is telling me, which is to be careful with her."

"Mom, Leanna has no reason to harm me. She doesn't like what's going on with me and Karl and she is trying to look out for me, too."

"Like what's going on with you and Karl?" she scoffed. "Lee, and I'm telling you, she shouldn't even know what's going on with you and him, period." Mom was stern.

"Okay, I understand." The girls had left the table to watch TV in the living area. "Mom, can I ask about your relationship with Leanna's mom?" I decided this might have been a good time to get more of the story. All I knew was when I was living with my dad, Helen, Leanna's mom had tracked my mom down and helped her get settled into a house to come get me. My father was so abusive to me; she wanted to help without him knowing.

Mom stopped stirring the gumbo, and with a sigh she muttered, "Go ahead, ask anything you want."

"Why did she decide to help you? She didn't even know you. Why would she give you money to get back on track?" I asked.

"You already know, so I could get you from your crazy dad. When she found me, I was still barely making it. To be honest, at first, she just wanted you out of her house. She said you caused too much chaos, and your dad was becoming physically abusive to her and was emotionally abusing you. She was afraid things would get worse for you. Apparently, your teacher had threatened to call the police, so she scrambled."

"Oh my God, you're talking about the teacher that did my hair and helped me at school." I finally knew that teacher did call the authorities because she knew I was being abused at home.

"Yes, so at first Helen was trying to save her own ass. When she found me and told me about what was going on with you, I was desperate to get you that same day. But she stopped me saying it had to be done right; she wanted to set me up to avoid you having to go back to their house." She took a deep breath and paused.

"Go on," I said.

"Well, as time went on, we actually developed a little friendship. She paid for our house up to a year, filled it with food and furniture, and bought us a car. She used some of your dad's money and he found out it was missing, he became suspicious. Then, his mother enters the picture; she finds out Helen was helping me and decides to help as well."

"Grandma Elizabeth?"

"Yes, between those two, our bills were paid for a while. But I still had to work and when that car broke down, it threw everything off. I hated to ask, but I actually called Helen before I called your dad…" Her voice got shaky, and she was hesitant to continue. "Me and Helen met, and she convinced me to call your dad and ask for some money, because after all, you were his child. She knew it would be a disaster if I did that. At first I refused to call him. She said to call, and she would try talking some sense into him to help me. Then before she left, she gave me a gun."

"No, no… Mom, she set you up!" I couldn't believe what I was hearing.

"It seems that way. But your dad was a hot head, and I fell into Helen's trap, I guess. Maybe we both fell into her trap. He was crazy and mean, but I had never imagined such aggression from him. It was like, someone gassed him up before coming to my house. When I was arrested for killing him, I believe it was Helen that paid for my lawyers. I know your Grandmother Elizabeth gave money to help support you while I was away. So, the neighbor you ended up with was paid to take care of you. She would have done it anyway, but the money helped. When I got out of jail, I had a nice house and car waiting on me, once again, from an anonymous person; I'm almost positive it was from Helen. She died from cancer several years later. That's all I got for you." I could tell she was done talking about it.

"Okay." I sat there, still bewildered by what Mom had said. Mrs. Ruiz came in and handed a sleepy Kaiden to me. I held him close, smelling his curly hair and admiring his green eyes. He was now close to eight months and a splitting image of his father. Kaiden was calm as if he knew I couldn't handle an overly demanding baby right now. He closed his eyes and immediately drifted to sleep.

I took Kaiden to his room and laid him down. Not wanting to leave him right away, I sat in the rocking chair by the window. I looked out over the backyard, still amazed at my home—at my life. The grass was well manicured with a line of beautiful trees at the end of the property. The freeform pool was framed with large decorative stones and a waterfall created with boulders and cascading plants. The extended pergola was outfitted with an outdoor kitchen, bar, and five table set ups. Karl and I loved entertaining out there and the girls loved playing on the massive swing set he designed for them. My home had six bedrooms and a mother-in-law suite my mom adored. Karl had given me a beautiful life. He was responsible for all the bills, and I saved and invested all the money left to me by Elizabeth Mohan, my dad's mother. He was so good to me; why couldn't I overlook all the bad feelings building up inside about him. Was I just being paranoid? Was it really just my hormones going crazy? Leanna was the only one that validated my feelings about Karl, but my conversation with Mom made me doubt her, too. I was so confused and felt like I had misjudged my relationship with Leanna—a relationship I desperately wanted.

CHAPTER 7

What Comes Around

Mike and I had been passing flirty DMs back and forth. Waves of guilt tortured me, but the more Karl came home late and distanced himself, the more I craved Mike's attention. I was falling back into my old thoughts of *'any attention is better than none.'* Going to the gym and caring for the kids kept me busy, but the late hours of silence and loneliness opened the door to the kind of forbidden communication that could disintegrate the strongest of marital fabric. I mistakenly opened up to Mike about my frustration and suspicion I had about Karl. Mike tried to play the supportive friend, but his opportunist ego wouldn't let him. He was attentive to my words and gently dragged me into this emotional affair. It was a matter of time before I ended up at his house. I was kind of curious to see how he lived because I had never been in his space. Everything in me warned against that visit, and I even called Karl hoping to come to my senses. As soon as he answered, he quickly said he would call me back. Right before he hung up, I heard a woman's laugh. I then drove to his office building, pulling up just in time to see him getting in his truck with Rachel. The urge to follow them was overshadowed by the desire to see Mike.

I walked into Mike's apartment with a knot in the pit of my stomach. I knew I shouldn't have been there and instantly felt terrible about my decision to come. The familiar smell of his cologne mixed with a sweet-smelling room spray relaxed me. *Ok Lee, just stay, chat, have one drink, and leave,* I told myself.

"Have a seat, make yourself at home," he said.

"Okay." I sat down still full of nervous energy.

"It's weird having you on my territory for once," he continued.

"Yea, very weird, and I'm the one that's married now," I said as a reminder to both of us.

"Ha… leave it to you to constantly remind us of who's married and who's not. I see some things haven't changed." He smiled.

"A lot has changed," I countered. "I'm also a mother and finally establishing a relationship with my half-sister. I'm particularly proud of that."

"Good for you." He handed me a glass of Crown and Coke. "Here you go, just like old times."

"Yes, but not quite."

"Right, I've never seen you nervous, Leesha. You're so shaky, it's funny. What are you scared of?"

"This, being here, makes me feel so wrong," I confessed.

"Technically, this is just a get together between old friends." He squinted his eyes and nodded his head like he was trying to convince himself that his words were true.

"Yes, friends." I followed his lead.

We finished our drinks with small talk of my kids and the stress of his wedding planning.

"I can't believe you're getting married again. She must be special." I dug for information.

"She is, but we met when I was at a weird place in my life. I had been divorced for almost two years, and was missing the benefits of having a wife, someone to talk to. I was also feeling bad about the cheating shit and breaking her fucking heart." He was staring off into space.

"You know, she came to my place after we stopped seeing each other," I said.

"Wait, what? My ex-wife came to your spot? What the fuck happened? Why didn't you tell me?"

"Yes, she did, and I didn't feel the need to tell you because we weren't talking anymore. She confronted me. I tried to lie but ended up kind of confessing, but not completely. I'll never forget the pain on her face... never."

"Wow, I had no idea that happened," he said.

"She basically said you were behaving like a cheating man, which was weird to me because we had stopped seeing each other. So, what or who were you doing after me?"

"I wasn't seeing anyone. I just wasn't coming home, that time I was actually staying at the office. I couldn't keep going home and listening to her jump all over me about my job and her family. I was still feelin' some kind of way after you ghosted me, and we had that last night together."

"Last sexless night, I will add."

"Right, it was sexless. That was the night I mentally let you go. That actually did fuck me up, but I'm sure you didn't care because you were moving on with Karl."

"Yup, now it seems like Karl is moving on, he is the one with the cheating behavior."

"He could have some shit on his mind and can't deal, like I did. But, you talking about that Rachel chick, right?"

"Yea, I saw her up in your face, too. Is she the office hoe or what?" I asked.

"Naw, she like to flirt, but she ain't my type. Believe me, ain't nobody fucking with her, I definitely don't think Karl is, regardless of the fact her ass is always in his face," he admitted.

"Right." I shook my head and tears unexpectedly filled my eyes.

"Hey, don't cry, please. I hate to see you sad like this. There's nothing I can say to make it better and I'm sorry."

"Not your fault, sometimes I think it's just karma," I admitted.

"Karma? What do you mean?" he asked.

"Obviously, because I messed with you and probably ruined your marriage. Now I got this young ass girl trying to ruin mine. What comes around goes around," I said.

"First off, my marriage was in trouble way before I met you. Me cheating, probably did put the nail in the coffin; or it could have been me just not even trying to make it right, not coming home and shit. If I would've tried, we would be together, and I would've still been listening to her nag me about working with her father."

"Do you regret cheating, meeting me and going through all that shit?" I asked.

"Hell no, I don't regret meeting you, being with you. Shit, me and you… fuck, we couldn't get enough of each other. I haven't met another Leesha Roberts, and I'm still crazy about you," he said, looking deep into my eyes.

Mike leaned in and slowly kissed me. A sensation that had laid dormant in my body slowly emerged, scaring me. The lingering need to feel seen and desired overcame me and I surrendered to his lips, hands, and his presence imposing on my sadness. I tried to fight the feelings and resist him.

"Stop it, get away from me." I pushed him off with the little strength I had left.

"No," he whispered and continued. Then he paused and looked in my eyes as if he were casting his spell on me like he'd done so long ago.

"I hate you," I breathed, leaning in for more.

"I hate you, too," he said as his lips traveled down to my neck overwhelming me with tongue filled kisses then back up to my mouth, slowly, deliberately sliding his tongue in as if he were poisoning me with whatever would release my inhibitions. Half my mind pleaded with me to stop, and the other half desired the attention. His hands traced down my back, sending chills throughout my body.

"Mike, I can't do this, it's not right. What about Karl?" I pleaded.

"He will never know."

"He will find out."

"No, he won't—unless you confess—but I can tell your body needs this as much as mine does. Let me do this for you, make you feel like the beautiful, sexy woman you are, please."

I was confused but my body was caving into the desire to feel Mike holding me. I was at the point where I needed to feel someone wanting me, worshiping my body, and Mike had no history of failing me in the bedroom.

He gently removed my shirt, exposing the black lace bra that overflowed with my full breasts. His eyes glimmered when he released my breasts letting them fall into his mouth, kissing and licking each one. I trembled with nerves and anticipation while his hands made their way to my pants, unbuttoning, unzipping, then sliding his fingers to my wet pussy. I gasped at the throbbing of my center as I responded to his touch, then I let out a guttural moan, once again letting him know that I needed this, that I wanted this. He got on his knees to peel off my tight jeans exposing my black lace panties. I was waiting for him to come back up and play with my breasts more because that was his pattern. Instead, I felt his finger slide into the side of my panties, exposing me. He gently massaged my clit, making me tingle all over, then he slowly licked my pussy. I tensed, surprised he was going there.

"My God, baby you taste so fucking good, I can't believe I was missing out on eating this pussy when we were together," he moaned and continued as if he were eating his last supper, savoring my pussy with every lick, kiss, and suck. Instinctively, my hands went to his head applying gentle pressure as I rolled my pussy on his tongue. He welcomed me, wrapping his arms around my thighs and pulling me closer to his face, encouraging my grind. My head fell back as he transported me to dangerous ecstasy. I laid there, shock waves traveling through my body making me tremble. "That's right, baby, ride that fuckin' wave," he encouraged my orgasm. Then he came back up, sliding his dick into my sensitive pussy.

"Yes, yes…" I was damn near begging him for more, accepting the fact I had already fallen from marital grace. He accepted my defeat and continued stroking me with rhythm that drove me crazy. "Oh God, oh God." My second orgasm summoned a scream.

"That's it, baby, let it all out," he encouraged me again. His pace quickened as he finally came.

We both laid there, breathless. My mind was racing, and I wondered what the fuck had I just done. The answer was… I had finally fulfilled my needs. Regrettably, I had done so at the possible expense of my family. My heart started pounding and the tightness in my chest made it difficult to breathe.

"I can't breathe." I clutched my chest; fully aware I was having a panic attack. "Mike, what did I just do, I ruined my life, oh my God."

"Leesha, calm down please. I know it's fucking scary, but I promise Karl ain't gonna know shit, so chill," Mike begged.

"I'm trying. Mike, I gotta go." I caught my breath and stood up, pulling on my clothes.

"Okay," he murmured, backing away from me. "Lee, I'm sorry. I was selfish because I never got you out of my system and I can't believe anyone would take you for granted. Please calm down before you leave."

"Really? There was a time you took me for granted," I mentioned.

"I know and that was the biggest mistake of my life, taking you for granted," he said.

"I don't believe that."

"I don't blame you; I understand. Forgive me." He walked closer and grabbed my face and slowly kissed me, breaking down my defenses once again. I kissed him back, telling myself this was our last time.

When I got home, it didn't surprise me Karl wasn't there. I took a shower and cuddled up with the girls in my bed and watched endless episodes of Gracie's Corner. Kaiden was in his crib laughing and enjoying the music, too. I was lost in thought, but the longer it took Karl to come home, the less guilt I felt about Mike. Karl stayed pissing me off. I wondered who he was with almost every evening.

A few hours later, the kids were in bed sound asleep. Karl came in and looked surprised I was sitting up reading. Well, I was acting like I was reading but I was still in a daze about my encounter with Mike. My guilt was somehow clouded in anger.

"Another late night?" I asked.

"Kinda, after we checked on the properties we went for drinks; celebrating the end of another tough week," he said matter-of-factly.

"Really? Who's we? If you don't mind me asking." I was just as nonchalant.

"Me and the guys."

"Not Rachel?"

"Please don't start. I said me and the guys. Please, I don't have the energy for your drama tonight. I'm getting in the shower." He shut the bathroom door. I hit the bed wishing it was him. He disregarded me so easily. I took two anxiety pills and drank a glass of wine, hoping to fall asleep as fast as possible. When he came out the bathroom, I felt him looking at me.

"Look, Lee, I'm sorry I keep blowing you off. But I'm tired of constantly defending myself when it comes to Rachel, who I have no inappropriate relationship with. I keep saying it and you keep accusing me. Don't you believe I love you? Don't you believe I would never do anything to hurt you, especially that." His words hit like a ton of bricks.

"I don't know how you expect me to feel. It seems like you constantly choose her over me, and you get angry when I bring it to your attention. I'm sorry, maybe I am a little sensitive. I had Kaiden, a traumatic hysterectomy, then you bring her in, it was all just too much."

"I understand and I'm sorry. Lee, I hate it when you're mad at me. It's so hard to come home and see the disappointment in your face." He crawled in bed and gave me a kiss. I winced at his touch. His face tensed and he backed away, looking at me as if he knew what I had just done. I was so fucking paranoid; I felt like he could smell Mike, saw his handprints all over me, and sensed his wife had been unfaithful. I shook it off and continued.

"I'm trying to make these feelings go away but I can't completely ignore my gut. Your actions are telling me something ain't right. If it is just me, then give me some time; if not, then you got some shit to figure out and you better hope and pray I don't find out." *Karl can say the same to me,* I thought, feeling like a complete hypocrite.

"Right… I'm not sure what to say. You won't believe anything at this point. I can't even touch you." He got out the bed and left the room, leaving me to deal with the crazy emotions and thoughts caused by suspicion and my irresponsible actions.

CHAPTER 8

Confrontations

Karl remained hot and cold. One minute he was Mr. Family Man and the next minute he couldn't be bothered with me or the kids. My efforts to be the loving wife that admittedly stemmed from the guilt of my encounter with Mike was going unnoticed by Karl. He was clearly preoccupied with something. Although I was now ignoring Mike, I still thought about him every day. His spirit had consumed mine, maybe because his touch had replaced Karl's. The more I thought about the whole situation, the angrier I got. Sure, I was mad at myself and felt guilt, but Karl was moving like he didn't care. He was always tired when he got home and never wanted to talk. So, after brunch and bottomless mimosas with Mikayla, I went to his office.

I knocked and walked in without an invitation, just like I had seen Rachel do so many times. Karl was sitting at his desk, and Rachel was sitting across from him with a notebook like she was taking notes.

"Lee, hey what's up," Karl said.

"I just came to see my husband," I announced.

"Okay, see me about what?" he asked. The anger was already rising in me.

"Do I need a reason? I mean, should I be asking Rachel if it's okay for me to come by your office?" I couldn't hold back. Karl threw down his pen and leaned back in his chair, hitting me with a challenging look. His eyes said, 'bring it on,' so I did. "Is that a way to look at your wife that gave birth to your three children? I come first, don't I?" Karl continued with a cold stare as I spoke. A cold look from a white man hits different; it makes any Black person furious. I guess the race issue was exaggerated because he was treating me like this in front of a white woman. I went around his desk and stood in front of him, blocking his view of Rachel.

"What Karl… you want me to leave? You're looking at me like you hate me. You sit here and humiliate me in front of this bitch!" I lost it. "I will drag you and her all over this fucking office! You two keep fucking with me, but you have no clue, I will fuck you up—acting like I don't belong in this space!" I turned toward Rachel who had already retreated to the door.

"You want me to call security?" she asked in a shaky voice. I walked toward her just to put a little more fear in her heart.

"Next time call security as soon as you see me for your safety because I'm done playing games with you. Leave my husband alone, and I mean it." I walked out.

&&& &&& &&&

Karl stormed into our bedroom and slammed down his keys, startling my mom and me.

"What the fuck is wrong with you? How dare you come to my job being fucking crazy and disrespectful?"

"Really, Karl? Go ahead and say it. How dare I come to the office being disrespectful to your bitch, Rachel. Have you fucking noticed you're always defending her?"

"What the fuck are you talking about? You're so threatened by her you can't see straight. You accused her of fucking me? That is crazy!"

"Why is it crazy? You don't touch me, you come home late, and any mention of sweet little Rachel, you lose your shit. You're always going somewhere with her," I shouted. Mom looked shocked, then started rubbing her face, surely trying to make sense of this.

"Well, let me call your ass out. You didn't feel it was necessary to confront her until you saw her in Michael Sinclair's face." My mom's eye shot up when he said that, and my heart fell to my stomach.

"What? What are you talking about?" I remained firm like he was being crazy. "What does Mr. Sinclair have to do with you and Rachel… and why would I care?"

"You mean Mike; ain't that what you call him? You fucking tell me why you would care." Karl was right in my face. "You know… I kept wondering, where the fuck I had seen Michael at. He looked familiar but I couldn't put my finger on it. Then I saw you two in the lobby that day we were planning the girls' party, and I fucking knew; I knew he was the one leaving your house that morning. You were angry at me for talking to my ex that night at the event when we were dating. He was the one who spent the night with you." Karl's eyes sparkled with rage; he kept walking toward me until he backed me up against the wall. My mom stood up and walked closer to us, ready to intervene. Karl did not let up. I felt desperate for this to end, and wanted him away from me, but I chose to stand my ground.

"You know what, Karl, if you want to deflect from what you got going on, then forget it. For all I fucking care, she can have either one of you," I screamed.

"Oh really, you gonna help her choose, Lee. You know us both so well." He finally backed off, but now I was the one walking up on him.

"No, Karl, she doesn't need my help choosing; it ain't that hard." My voice was cold. I glared at him and immediately knew I had made a mistake, but I wanted to hurt him like he was trying to hurt me. He slowly backed away with a look of disgust on his face, picked up his keys, and left.

"Child, what did you just do?" My mom's voice broke the silence.

"I don't know, Mom. I just don't know." This time, my pride stopped the threat of tears.

Karl had started sleeping in the guest bedroom. I was beyond upset and wasn't sure if I was mad at him or myself. I had to remember he was the one withholding affection; he was the one with suspicious behavior. I could admit not being an angel in this situation, and welcoming the inappropriate flirtation Mike offered me. I also regretted our adulterous encounter, but Karl's bullshit made it difficult for me to feel bad about it. I had made peace with the fact I had slept with Mike, and it was a mistake. But punishing myself wasn't going to help anything. The fact is, that was going to be something I would never admit, and I'd plan on taking it to my grave. The only thing that made Karl leery was I didn't tell him I knew Mike. But why should I? I'm sure some of the ladies at these parties we went to were from his past and he probably fucked a few, but he wasn't telling me which ones. That shit didn't matter because we were married; we chose each other. But now it seemed like he was choosing someone else. I didn't have any solid proof, just my woman's intuition that something was going on. I hated us being in the same house and not talking.

"Karl… I need you to talk to me." I had made my way to the guest room late one night.

"We can't let this happen to us; we have children." The silence was deafening. "Karl please, my heart hurts so bad." I continued to fight the tears that inevitably filled my eyes. He finally responded, reaching up to take my hand and pulled me close to him. I laid on his chest and relief embraced me along with his arms. "I want you to know that there is nothing between Mike and me. He was part of my past and that's all. Never would I expect for him to work with you, and—" Karl squeezed me tighter.

"Lee, just be quiet, I don't want to hear this." He cut me off.

"Okay, but just let me say, I love you so much, with everything in me, and I could never hurt you. Tell me you know that."

"Yes, I know." That was all he said. I noticed he did not tell me the same. Once again, no reassurance at all. My heart broke even more.

CHAPTER 9

Secret Rivalry

After that night, Karl returned to our bedroom. We made love more often and he was becoming more attentive. But something was still off. I had already confronted Rachel, so what more could I do. It might sound crazy, but I went to Karl's grandmother, Francine, for advice. She was the one that hooked me and Karl up and was always straight with me. I knocked on her door at Lotus Gardens, the place I used to manage full-time before I had the girls. She answered wearing the same black lounging dress with silver trim she wore years ago when she read my cards for the first time. She walked a bit slower now but was still her spunky self. I told her everything that had been happening with me and Karl.

"You need to be at peace with yourself. This inner turmoil is not good for you and will not help at all. If you want the truth revealed just ask. Matter of fact, it's a full moon tonight. Go outside and just sit under that moon, calm yourself. Pray and ask for truth and understanding. After that, release it, and know you will get your answers." She gave advice in the typical Francine style. But I needed that because I had to believe in something other than myself.

"Okay, I will. I'm scared of being hurt when I find out. I hope it's nothing, and it's all in my mind," I confessed.

"Stop it," she demanded. "You're not crazy and don't let anyone make you believe stuff is all in your head. I know Karl is my precious grandson, but men are men. They make you think you're losing your mind. Quite frankly, if you feel this deeply, you have your answer already. It may not be the exact answer, but you have it. Be strong, you have kids, and you have your own damn money, my dear," she reminded me of the money I had inherited from Grandma Mohan.

I thought back to the reading of the will, which initially caused a lot of upset with Leanna and the rest of my dad's family. Eventually Leanna came around and we started working on our relationship. I was grateful for that, at least I would have her support too if something happened with me and Karl. Francine continued to speak as if she were privy to things about my life I hadn't divulged. I had found out long ago she had more gifts than reading cards.

"I can imagine you are feeling a little unseen by Karl with all his working and, not to mention, this woman that is now working there." She shocked me with that comment. I had never thought about the fact that I did feel unseen and unheard.

"Yes," I answered. "I do feel ignored and invisible."

"You are craving attention, and there seems to be someone willing to give it to you. But that could be costly. You understand, right?" The slow nod of her head kind of creeped me out.

"I'm not sure what you mean," I lied.

"Don't worry, dear, I'm the last one to judge you." She laughed. Now, I was just nervous.

"Things are never what they seem, be careful of who you let into your life. Also, that man has never gotten over you. Be careful with him; he could be more trouble than you can handle. As for your sister, the less said, the better." She gave me a lot to think about.

I left Francine's feeling more unsettled than before.

It was 9 p.m. and Karl was not home. I sat by the pool with a glass of wine, enjoying the silence of the night accompanied by the full moon. Anger and sadness overwhelmed me, but I remembered Francine said I had to release all that and be at peace before I asked for the clarity I needed. So, I did what I felt like I had been doing for days… I cried just to get it all out. Then I prayed for God to take this heaviness away. Finally, there was a strange feeling that overcame me—calm, peace, and acceptance. I looked at the moon and uttered, "Please reveal the truth and understanding I need." I took a deep breath and let it go.

Karl got home around 11:30 p.m. He took a shower and quietly slid into bed. He thought I was asleep, so I just laid there—heart breaking. But I was confident everything would be revealed soon.

The next morning, I was sitting at the kitchen table when Karl got downstairs.

"You got in late last night," I said.

"Yea, I'm sorry. One of the contractors fell through for a big project and we had to go through more bids to get the paperwork together for another one," he answered.

"Oh, okay." I wondered if "we" were him and Rachel. I also wondered if Mike was there. But I decided not to ask. "Please try to get home earlier, the kids are looking for you before bed. You need to at least be around to say goodnight to them." I took a sip of coffee, trying to look unbothered.

"Okay." He leaned over and kissed me on the forehead. "See you later, have a good day."

"Bye." I was trying to stay calm, but I was tired of being taken for granted.

It was weeks later, and everything was still the same. I thought back of when Mike and I had our affair and after it was over his wife came to my door. Now I understood the devastation that was on her face, I understood the pain she carried, and how difficult it must have been to come to my house. I guess karma was kicking my ass now because all I did was sit and wonder what the hell my husband was doing. Karl had called and said he would be late again. I called Mikayla and asked to borrow her car. I had decided to follow him. I had to know what was going on. *Okay universe, I will get my own answers.*

I parked down the street from his office building close to 5 p.m., waiting for him to come out. First person I recognized was Mike walking out, looking good as hell. He hopped into his Range Rover and left. Half an hour later, Rachel and Karl came walking out. They waved goodbye and went their separate ways. No affection was observed. Maybe they were playing it cool. Karl pulled off hitting the 410 ramp and Rachel looped around to the side road. I followed Karl. After driving nearly thirty minutes, he pulled into a Marriot near Six Flags. What in the world was he doing here? The glass doors and huge windows offered me a clear view to the lobby. I saw him walk in and not stop at the front desk. I was going to be forced to get out. I waited twenty minutes then went in.

"Hi, where is the conference room please?" I asked the man at the front desk.

"We have three conference rooms, ma'am. They are all closed. There are no meetings scheduled for this evening." He smiled.

"Oh okay. Do you have a reservation for Karl Michaels. He is expecting me," I said with a nervous smile.

He gave me a suspicious look. "Ma'am, we don't give information out about guests, sorry."

I took a deep breath and tears filled my eyes. "Please, do you have a Karl Michaels registered here?" He sighed and looked down at the computer.

"No, there are no reservations for a Karl Michaels." He gave me a look of pity.

"Thank you." I hurried out. When I got to the car I sat there contemplating my next move. The only option was to sit and wait for him to come out. My heart pounded and I thought about going in and knocking on every door, screaming Karl's name, but I had more dignity than that. I shut my eyes tight and opened them after giving myself a pep talk. As soon as they opened, I saw a familiar woman walking through the parking lot with an Olive Garden bag. My heart stopped and I screamed when I saw who it was. Leanna walked through the glass door, waved at the clerk, and headed to the elevators. My sister… what was she doing here? Why didn't she tell me she was in town? Why was she meeting my husband? I jumped out the car and ran into the lobby. The clerk looked up and realized who I was after. He looked at the elevator then back at me.

"Ma'am, if you are not a guest, you can't go up." He came around the desk to stop me

"I..I, please, please help.." All words were escaping me. I started crying and shaking. He wrapped his arms around me as I cried uncontrollably. There I was, suffering through public humiliation, getting comforted by a stranger. Why was this happening to me? *God, please make this pain stop.*

After sitting outside the hotel for another hour in a full-blown breakdown, calling Karl and getting no answer, anger overtook me, and I called Leanna. She answered the phone so cool and casual. I matched her energy.

"Hey, Lee," she answered.

"Hey, Leanna. Guess where I am?" I said.

"What? Where are you, sister?" The nerve of her to call me that.

"I'm right outside the Marriot that you and Karl are at. Do me a favor and tell him to get his ass out here before I burn this whole muthafucka down." My voice was calm enough for her to know I was serious. I hung up the phone, got out the car, and waited by the door.

Exactly two minutes later, Karl walked out the door and I punched him in the face. He stumbled back.

"What the fuck!" he said, wiping the blood from his nose.

"What the fuck are you doing here with my sister?" I screamed.

"Lee, let's go home, please." He immediately started to beg.

"You ain't got a home, you son of a bitch!" I got so close to his face; I could smell his blood. "Do you know I will kill you? You have no idea who you fuckin' with," I sneered.

"Oh, the apple doesn't fall too far from the tree. You gonna kill him, right. Like your mother killed my father?" Leanna had come out of nowhere. I charged at her, but Karl grabbed me.

"Lee, stop it! Not here, not now," Karl pleaded.

"Karl, don't talk to me!" I warned him.

"Oh, Karl, baby let her go. Leesha Renée, how does it feel not to have it all anymore? How does it feel to have the most important person ripped out of your hands, little miss perfect?" Leanna's voice was mocking. This was all a big game to her. My life and family were destroyed just for her to prove a point.

"I never want to see your face again," I said to Leanna. "You did what you came to do." She laughed loudly. I charged her again and Karl grabbed me. "Let me go! You two are not worth it! Karl, you need to go to the house, get all your shit, and leave. Looks like you'll be living at the Marriot." I stormed away.

Karl's truck was already at home by the time I got there. It had taken me a while to drop off Mikayla's car. She had seen the devastation on my face, but I couldn't bring myself to tell her what I had discovered. I walked in the house trying to act as normally as possible and asked Mrs. Ruiz if she could spend the night with the kids and she agreed. When I got to the bedroom, Karl was sitting there waiting.

"Get the fuck out, I'm done talking to you." I was calm, there were no more tears left to cry.

"Leesha, I was not, nor did I ever sleep with your sister," he started. "I made the mistake of confiding in her about what we were going through, next --thing I know she's in town asking to meet."

"That makes zero sense! I don't expect you to admit to sleeping with her, but I know better. As for that confiding shit, Karl, I've been here for you to talk to me. You were the one never available—too busy chasing ass. How could you, with my own sister?"

"Leesha, I was not sleeping with your sister!" he yelled.

"Liar!" I walked into the bathroom and slammed the door. He opened it before I could lock it.

"Lee, please just listen to me." Tears filled his eyes. "I need you to believe me. I was not having an affair with Leanna. Please!" He slipped to the floor and wrapped his arms around my legs, restraining me from any movement. He was so desperate and pathetic. "Lee, you know I wouldn't do that to you, we have a family; what about our kids," he begged.

"Kids? You mean the ones that I just asked you to come home to at least tell them goodnight. My life has been turned upside down, I struggled mentally and physically, and you needed someone to confide in? I don't get it." I remained calm. Karl loosened his grip and sat on the floor. I couldn't stand the sight of him.

"I love you and my kids. You are the best thing that has ever happened to me, and I don't know why I didn't just come to you. I didn't want to burden you with my feelings when you were dealing with yours. I'm sorry; I fucked up.

"Karl, get up, just leave, get out of my face. Please give me some time," I said.

"No, you have to say you believe me. I can't let your time be filled with thoughts that I was sleeping with your sister. I can't have you think that about me. Please let me explain."

"There is nothing you can say that will explain you meeting my sister at a hotel. You walked in there like you knew exactly where to go; like it wasn't a new thing. I can't listen to you right now, please just leave me alone." I stepped over his legs and walked back into our bedroom, put on pajamas, got into bed, and covered my face. I heard Karl walk out and the door shut.

"Hello," Leanna's cheerful voice stunned me. I had a feeling this call wasn't going to go as planned.

"Why? Why did you mess with Karl? Why would you ruin my family?" My voice was shaky.

"Why not?" Her answer sent me into a rage.

"Listen, you worthless bitch; my husband will never want you. He used you for a piece of ass and you were stupid enough to give it to him." I had already lost control.

"Really, from our hours of pillow talk, it seemed to be more than just wild, hot passionate sex. Believe me, it was hot. My pussy is wet just thinking about it," she continued to taunt me.

"How could you? You are a crazy bitch!" I screamed.

"Why not! You and your mother took everything away from me. She killed my father. Yes, I admit he wasn't the greatest person, but he was good to me. Then my mother died surely from the guilt of having him murdered, leaving me with my grandmother. Then, my grandmother left almost everything to you! You got everything because she felt sorry for you. It was ridiculous. I couldn't stand it; seeing you live a perfect life when almost everything was taken from me. So yes, I decided to disrupt your perfect life." She sounded so evil and crazy.

"Leanna, I need to know if you really did sleep with Karl. I know you hate me and quite frankly, I hate you too now, but if you have any ounce of decency, you will tell the truth." I needed to know how to go on with my marriage.

"I already told you that." She laughed.

"The truth, I need the truth; not words to just hurt me." I found myself pleading with her.

She quietly spoke. "You'll never know, live with it, Leesha, Goodbye." She hung up. My heart broke from the fact I indeed would have to live without knowing and with the fact I had lost my sister again, this time it was for good.

I felt so miserable after talking to her. I walked around in a fog for days. Depression had overtaken me again and the medication had ceased working. I was heartbroken and Karl stayed with 'I didn't sleep with her, I just confided in her' story. He did start coming home either on time or early. But nothing he did or said could bring me out of the hole my mind lived in. Mrs. Ruiz was practically living here and caring for the kids. I had no one to talk to; there was no way I was going to tell my mother. Mikayla had just gotten engaged, and I wanted her to enjoy her happiness without my bullshit crowding up her space again.

The depression brought thoughts of Johnathon. He was the one I wanted to talk to. When Karl and my sister weren't on my mind, Johnathon was. I still couldn't believe he was dead. There had been no sign that he was looking over me—no more dreams, no white birds, or stray feathers. I prayed to God for peace, one way or the other. The pain and disappointment were killing me and quite frankly, I wished it would hurry up. Also, I had to face my own indiscretions with Mike. My guilt begged me to forgive Karl. After all, if I forgave him and my shit ever surfaced, maybe he could forgive me, too. But my sister… and they were meeting at a hotel. The confiding claims made me believe that their shit was emotional, and it was planned. Oh God, why me! This was such a mess.

I grabbed the mirrored box from my bedside table, opened it, held it to my face, inhaling deeply, hoping the smell would bring me comfort. Johnathon had left the box when he moved away, and it had been long emptied of the weed we used to smoke together. It now held pictures of me and Johnathon. I laid down and held the box tight, falling into yet another fitful sleep.

Awakened by the box crashing on the floor, I jumped up to see it had only broken into a few pieces. I quickly picked up the pictures and noticed a folded piece of paper that had been somehow hidden underneath the floor of the box. My heart pounded as I opened it. I gasped when I saw Johnathon's handwriting.

> *Leesha,*
>
> *So, you really broke our box? That's why we can't have nice things, LOL. I want you to know I miss you every day, even in death. Whatever worries or disappointments you go through, just know you are strong enough to handle it and you are great in every way. I hope you enjoy your life and learn to look at blessings and not disappointments. One thing for sure is you will die one day, and I hate for you to have lived a life focused on the negative. In whatever you face be strong, be happy, and be present. There is no need to know or fix everything because in the end, it's really not that serious. Have fun, love, live, and remember your worth. Hopefully you will have children one day and you can show them what strength and grace looks like. Love you forever,*
>
> *Johnathon*

It was like he was there with me, and I found this letter at the perfect time. I had so many emotions reading it. I laughed and cried, but sadness wrapped itself around me again. I finally let out the scream that had been lingering in my soul for so long.

CHAPTER 10

Emotionless Connections

The discovery of Karl and Leanna still weighed heavily on me. I felt like I was buried in a sand box of emotions. Every time I tried to dig my way out, more debilitating thoughts would cover me. No matter how hard I tried to be positive and move on like Johnathon's letter said, I just couldn't. I still hadn't told anyone about what I discovered that day because I still needed time to process it without someone else in my ear. I also feared having to admit that Karl wasn't the only cheater in this relationship. The secrets in this marriage threatened the fabric of our seemingly strong bond. I went to Karl again, looking for the truth.

"Karl, I really need you to tell me the truth. I know it may be hard for you, but it's not fair for me to not know. You say you didn't sleep with Leanna, but my gut is saying something different. I admit I have been hard for you to confide in, and my emotions may have caused some distance between us, but we can't go on without the truth. Please baby, just tell me." I ran my fingers through his hair. I had decided I would get more out of him turning the tables and taking some responsibility. But I knew better than to believe that me, or my emotions caused this.

"Lee, I don't.. I can't do this right now," he stuttered.

"Why, it's just us here. Karl this is me and you; we love each other, right? We can't have this shit hanging over us." I kept my voice calm.

"Leesha, I love you so much and I can't stand the thought of losing you." Karl finally looked me in the eyes. I felt my heart squeeze and took deep breaths to steady my trembling. My body knew what was coming, but I was still scared to hear it.

Karl lifted his finger and slowly uttered the words, "One time." I slipped to my knees and grabbed my chest. I gasped, inhaled, and choked on the flood of salty tears. Karl kneeled down and held me. "I made a mistake, and I am so sorry. Never in my life would that ever happen again." I opened my mouth, but no words would come out. "Please forgive me," he begged.

"My sister, how could you, with her? At the hotel, was that supposed to be a second time?"

"No, no, I wasn't going to let that happen again."

"But you were there. When did you and her do this the first time?" I needed particulars now.

"It doesn't matter, Lee. All that matters is it won't happen again."

"It should've never happened," I shot back.

"I know. We had been talking on the phone about you, then she came in town for a medical conference and wanted to meet up. I agreed and one thing led to another. It was just sex, nothing more, no feelings, nothing, I promise." His voice was shaky.

"Just sex… right," I mumbled as I shook my head. Karl held me as I continued to cry.

Coping with Karl's confession caused me to fall into old toxic habits. Mike was still living in my head and constantly in my DMs. Since I had come to the realization my husband had been sleeping with my sister, I decided it wouldn't be a complete sin if I did start answering Mike's messages. Of course that made me just as bad as Karl, but I had never given off the impression that I was the bigger person. Matter of fact, I always say, "when they go low, I go lower." Mikayla would laugh at me saying, "I could never be a Michelle Obama." So, I once again made the mistake of entertaining Mike's conversation. Yes, it was purely because I wanted that reassurance I was still desirable, still good enough.

After debating with Mike for at least a month, I found myself at his place again. He welcomed me in with a strong drink. Then he pulled out a bag of weed and papers.

"Wait a minute… you smoke?" I was surprised.

"Yea, on very rare occasions. My nephew left it here last weekend and they don't drug test us at work. But you smoke, too, don't you?" He looked at me as if he knew all my secrets.

"No," I said.

"But you used to because that last night I came to your house, you were high as fuck." He laughed. "So, smoke with me." He gave me a sly smile, making me want to run out the door.

"No, I'm good. You go ahead, though," I said. He nodded his head and lit the thinly rolled blunt.

Whatever he had given me to drink made me overly comfortable and my lips loose. I told him about Karl and my sister. He sat there shocked for a second.

"Naw, Karl loves your fuckin' dirty drawers. That dude ain't going nowhere."

"Well, it's true and he did go somewhere else."

"True that, I guess you right then," he said, knowing that this shit was playing in his favor.

"Anyway, how are the wedding plans going?" I asked. Mike's face tensed and he took a deep breath.

"It's going okay, I guess. She really wants a big wedding and not hearing what I gotta say. But I understand, she's never been married before."

"Are you sure you ready to be married again? I mean, you are sitting here with me."

"Yea, and I can basically say the same thing to you," he countered.

"You could. I am well aware I have no business being here with you. I mean, you've never been good for me. Our relationship always consists of infidelity; first yours, now mines. It's like God keeps warning us to stay away from each other." I rolled my eyes and sighed, simply disgusted with the fact I was sitting there. Mike must have sensed he was losing ground with me.

"Or maybe God is saying, 'shit, y'all need to just get together.' I mean we always keep coming back to each other. We gotta good vibe, just our timing sucks."

"Yea, we get along and gotta good vibe, but I'm letting you know, you are the biggest narcissistic asshole ever."

"Wow! Tell me what you really think about me! You hurt my feelings." He grabbed his chest. "I get it, though. I never showed you the real sensitive me, cause you broke me. I didn't want you to get to me because you low-key was making me crazy. All that bravado shit was my way of protecting my heart and honestly my marriage." His honesty caught me off guard.

"I don't know if I believe that," I said.

"You can believe it. You're that woman that got away, or the one I want and can never have." He looked away and took a drag of the half smoked blunt. Staring at the floor, he continued. "That night you had a fight with Karl, and I came over, I told you that I loved you, and I fucking meant that shit. When I saw you again…"

"Stop it now, no feelings, no love shit, no emotions. I can't deal with that. I don't want that. I'm here because I like the attention you give me; I like the fact that you chase me. I'm using you to feed my wounded ego, that's all." My words were hurtful to keep both our feelings at bay.

"Okay, so who's the narcissistic asshole now? Damn…" He quickly finished his drink.

"So that's what it is then, no emotions. I get it, I can follow directions and play my position. So, you want attention? I can give your body all the attention it needs, no emotion… I promise." He looked at me and we both laughed nervously.

"Do it then. I don't know what you been waiting for," I said. We stopped laughing and stared at each other. Mike looked down as to have a moment of thought then he took another drag, turned toward me, and slowly blew the smoke toward my lips. I responded by opening my mouth and inhaling deeply. With my eyes now closed, I felt his hand gently circle my neck. The rest of the smoke entered and was followed by his lips. That kiss was so passionate, so nasty—I felt like he was already fucking me. He backed away, causing my body to jolt back to reality.

"What? You scared to back up that kiss you just gave me?" My voice was calm, but my body was eager to experience his kiss again.

"Naw… I don't need you getting all crazy on me. I mean we both said this ain't serious, right? We gonna keep fucking? Eventually, this can get messy," he said.

"No messier than it already is. Besides, we're just having fun, right." I was still asking for trouble.

"I see it in your eyes, sometimes you want more, but too chicken shit to say it, especially after I put this dick on you again." Yeah, Mike was definitely overly confident.

"Wow, you're a trip, for real." I didn't know if he was bragging on himself or insulting me.

"But… I know how to fuck you and make sure you don't catch feelings."

"What are you even talking about?" I was intrigued.

Mike grabbed my neck again, slowly licked my lips, and followed it up with another debilitating kiss. "I can just fuck you. I can just tie your ass up and fuck you. When I get done, you will be satisfied, but no feelings caught, I promise, not the way I'm gonna do you. You gonna let me do it, Lee?" he asked.

"Oh yes, I'll let you do whatever. Um… am I gonna need a safe word or something?"

"Fuck no; I know what I'm doing." He was confident and I was curious.

We went to his room, and I just stood there, not knowing what to do. Mike came closer to me, the look in his eye more domineering than anything. He slowly got on his knees and said, "Open those fuckin' legs." He lifted my left leg, resting it on his arm as he raised my bodycon dress and pulled my panties to the side. "You got a pretty pussy." He rubbed it, making my legs tremble then followed it with a long, firm lick, just enough to tease me. He got up, went to the drawer, took out two condoms, and two sets of handcuffs before taking his clothes off. His body was muscular, perfectly chiseled. He had a mole on the right side of his lower groin, right above his perfectly manscaped dick. It was long, thick, hooked to the left, beautiful like a work of art. It stood straight up, the weight causing it to bob like a float in water. I wanted to turn and run but refused to chicken out. He threw everything on the bed and proceeded to take my dress off. His calculated moves took the giddy feeling of intimacy away, just like he said. His slow approach made me believe there was going to be some passion, but instead he grabbed me and forcibly turned me around and pushed me against the wall, lifted my leg, and positioned himself behind me. I fought back a scream from the instant pressure and pain as he entered me. The beat of his throbbing dick sent waves through my pussy, beckoning her to release the creamy essence that had built up.

"Ah yes, ahhh…" I couldn't even get a good moan out, each stroke was deeper, harder, more aggressive. Suddenly, he pulled out—dick glistening from my saturated pussy. "No, no," I begged him to come back.

"Lay on your back, spread eagle, baby." He pointed toward the bed. I did as instructed, and he secured both arms to his headboard, and left my legs free. My heart was ready to explode with fear and anticipation. My nipples hardened with arousal and the room's chill. I squirmed, wanting him to blanket my anxious body. He lifted my legs and positioned himself in the center, slowly rubbing his dick up and down my pussy, painfully teasing me.

"Don't play with me," I moaned, attempting to slide my hips closer to him, but was stopped by the handcuffs, causing my body to jerk.

"Easy, baby, good things come to those who wait." His words and dick taunted me. He gradually entered me, pleasuring me with torturous strokes. I finally relaxed and succumbed to whatever was to come next. I closed my eyes, becoming lightheaded from the rhythm of his dick.

"Yea, get drunk off that dick, keep them eyes closed." I felt him squeezing my neck. Instinctively, I yanked on the cuffs as his grip tightened and pace quickened. Hips now lifted and knees cradling the sides of my head, he dove deeper, bringing an uncontrollable painful pleasure to my entire body. Finally satisfied, my guttural moans announced one of the best orgasms I'd ever had. Suddenly, Mike had the upper hand and the grin on his face told me he knew it.

CHAPTER 11

Marriage Recovery

For the next few weeks, I tiptoed around the house hoping to conceal the fact I had been with Mike again. Karl was still overly apologetic, and frankly I wasn't even pressing him about it because I had my own shit to deal with. I had concluded Karl fell into my sister's trap. Still no excuse, and the same went for me. We slowly started talking more to each other. Of course, we were there for the kids and during those times of playing and loving on them we forgot all of our troubles. We would look at each other and remember there was love there and it wasn't just for the kids. Karl and I had made a mess of our union, but we loved each other. One night, I was cuddled on the couch watching a marathon of Tubi movies. He came in the living room catching a glimpse of an over done husband and wife scene.

"Tubi?" he asked, well aware of my Sunday movie marathons.

"Yes," I answered. Surprisingly, he grabbed a beer and joined me on the couch. I stretched my leg over his lap, and he started to massage my foot. It felt like old times. We watched silently for about an hour before he turned to me.

"Lee, I want to talk to you," he said.

"Okay." My heart pounded, afraid of what he was going to say.

"I'm not gonna start talking about your sister again; it's very clear that I fucked up. But I want to know if you are willing to fight for our marriage because I can't be here living life, raising kids with just a roommate. I want what we had back, and I can't do it myself. I need you to say that you still want this, that you still want us." His words gave me some relief and finally some insight on what he was thinking.

"I feel the exact same way. I want us… I want this life with you and our babies, and I really do still and always will love you, Karl." I had been waiting to say those words to him because no amount of anger could stop my heart from aching for him.

"I love you too, Lee." He leaned in and we were kissing when Lizzie and Frankie came in.

"Uck, so nasty, Daddy!" Lizzie yelled.

"Mommy no kiss Daddy no more!" Frankie chimed in. Karl and I looked at each other and laughed. I put my head on his shoulder, and we held hands.

Karl and I started counseling a week later. My previous therapist, Ms. Franklin, had referred us to Mr. Lordes, a marriage counselor. After all the formalities were done, Mr. Lordes said what I knew was coming, but it still scared me.

"What is most important in these sessions is that you two commit to being completely honest with each other. You both voiced some suspicions about infidelity. Once we get those questions answered we can talk about the whys. I want to be clear, there will be no blaming, finger pointing, or accusing. Leesha, you seem to be more open to talking, so you go first. Tell me about the birth of your son."

"First, I want to make it clear that I love my son so much. But he is what turned my world upside down. His birth was much more difficult than the girls, and they are twins. I passed out right after having him, I didn't get that immediate bonding moment. Next thing I know, I woke up, chest hurting and stomach in pain from what I thought was from the delivery. But then I was told that I had an emergency hysterectomy; not only that, but I also coded and needed CPR. I… I died, and that was scary. My kids could have been without a mother and Karl.. Karl." I started to cry. Karl embraced me, comforting me as I gathered my composure.

"Karl, what was going on in your mind when all that was happening to your wife?" Mr. Lordes asked the most obvious question; a question I should have asked him over a year ago.

"Terrified, guilty, like it was all my fault. My wife could have died. Hell, she did die. The girls were so young, and I pushed her into getting pregnant again so soon. I convinced her that it would be a good idea to have our kids close together. She agreed, probably just to make me happy, but her body wasn't ready. I almost lost the love of my life. It was traumatic to see her laying there and the doctor pumping frantically on her chest, everyone running around, trying to save her life, and I stood there frozen in fear, not doing anything." He balled his trembling hand into a fist to get control. His shaky voice continued. "What kind of man can't do anything to help his wife, then allow them to take her uterus on top of everything else. Lee was so sad when she found out I let them do that, but I had no choice. I didn't have time to think anything through and her mom was going crazy saying they were trying to kill her, and they didn't care because she was just another Black woman. When they stabilized her, the doctor hit us with the hysterectomy shit. Her mom lost it and started screaming *'of course you want to take her uterus, who cares if a Black woman is able to have kids again!'* I had to wrap my mind around all that noise and try to make the right decision for my wife. Lee doesn't know all that went on because her mental state was so fragile for so long. I always wondered if I should have asked for another doctor, a better doctor to control the bleeding, I always wondered if what her mom said was true about my wife being treated differently because she was Black. But I knew deep down that the doctor wanted nothing more but to save her life and I know he did the right thing. That don't stop my guilt though… I just needed to talk to someone, anyone." His voice trailed off afraid to say what was coming next.

I was upset I had never asked what happened, upset my mom had put Karl in that position. My mom could be overly emotional and irrational at times… just like me. I did not know the guilt and the doubt Karl had been carrying around because I was too selfish to ask. All I had been worried about was how he made me feel. I did not understand he couldn't maintain the capacity to constantly deal with my emotions. Instead, I accused, yelled, fought, cried, anything to rationalize what I eventually ended up doing too… cheating. Oh my God, I played a huge part in ruining this marriage.

"Leesha got depressed, that was my fault, too. I tried to bring help in the home, and again, another bad idea. I couldn't do anything right, so I just started staying away, but I love my wife, and I would always rather be with her," he admitted.

"How do you feel about what you just heard your husband say?" Mr. Lordes asked.

"I'm sad and upset that he had to go through all that, especially what my mom put him through. I had no idea what happened. My mom was raising hell, and my husband was falling apart. I'm so sorry, and you did the right thing, Karl. I was never angry at you about the decisions you made. I'm sorry for everything I did, and everything I said," I apologized. I did have a fleeting thought of confessing my indiscretions but quickly came to my senses. Karl had not explained his loyalty and attachment to Rachel, and sleeping with my sister was unforgivable. That was too much for me, so I was saving my confession time until I was ready. But I was still sorry and wished he would have told me all this before, but it was my fault too because I never asked about his emotions. For that, I took full responsibility.

The next few sessions consisted of us talking more about our feelings and learning how to communicate. Sometimes I would speak and the guilt of my encounters with Mike would be apparent in my voice. Mr. Lordes would look at me as if he knew, eyes squinting trying to catch a glimpse of the visions of me and Mike in my head. I didn't see that Karl got the same look, even though he was the one caught red-handed. Mr. Lordes made it clear that we each had to take responsibility for our own actions and not wait on the other to accept the ultimate blame for our marital woes.

Karl and I were almost back to normal, but we had moments of discord from things left unsaid. I guess we both had decided that we would live with whatever secrets that threatened our union. Yes, we decided to forgive the unknowingly unforgivable.

Dangerous Confessions

I t was time for the annual charity event. I remember the first time I went to this event; Karl and I argued over his ex, and I left early. That was the night Mike had come over and he had finally accepted that we were over. That was also when Karl had seen Mike leaving my house the next morning. I was snapped out of my thoughts when I felt Kaiden clinging to my leg. He was already one, and the girls were getting ready to turn four. Kaiden was walking but he didn't talk much. Between me and his sisters he didn't have to say much; we all catered to him. Mrs. Ruiz came in and grabbed Kaiden's hand.

"Mommy played with you all day, let her get dressed now." He protested for a minute but was eventually lured away with promises of milk and animal cookies. The girls sat in front of the TV watching *Princess and the Frog*. Lizzie was wearing her princess costume again and Frankie was in a long T-shirt, shorts, and cowboy boots. Karl was already dressed and sitting on the couch watching the movie with the girls and drinking whisky.

I wore a white sequin halter top dress with a rhinestone and pearl purse with shoes to match. My hair was straightened and pulled into a sleek ponytail. Everything was set off by my long sparkly earrings. Karl showered me with compliments, and I returned the sentiments because he looked sexy as hell in his black suit and black Stetson cowboy hat. All that black highlighted his shiny green eyes.

This year there were more people than normal and to my surprise there was finally more diversity in the crowd. Mike was there with his fiancé. I hadn't seen or talked to him in over two months and his wedding was in three months. They sat at the table next to ours and Mike couldn't keep his eyes off me. By now, Mike's attention on me was less than subtle, staring at me with his fiancé hanging on his arm. Mikayla, who sat at my table, was becoming more irritated. Karl was busy socializing with all the eventgoers, and finally I asked Mikayla to go outside because Mike made me uncomfortable. We were outside for about five minutes before Mike followed and fiancé was nowhere in sight. He walked up and Mikayla got between us already defensive. She knew about our past but didn't know our slip ups after Karl and I were married. But she knew Mike could easily throw me off balance.

"Not too much, Mike; you're doing the most, and you're gonna ruin her life, so just stop it!" Mikayla demanded.

"I just wanna talk to her. I ain't trying to ruin shit," he protested. Mikayla sucked her teeth and walked away.

"Mike, what do you want? Your fiancé is right next to you, Karl is right there, and you are staring at me like a crazy man." My face grew red with anger.

Mike took a sip of his drink. "I just want to talk to you." He tapped my chest as he spoke. He was obviously drunk.

"No, Mike." I backed away.

"I can't stand to see you with him." His intoxicated eyes glistened with sadness cut with a hint of anger.

"You mean my husband whom I love and whom I have three children, not to mention your client!"

"This shit is making me crazy," he continued.

"Well, don't get crazy just concentrate on your fiancé and your upcoming wedding; remember you're getting married, remember like you were married when we first met."

"You don't think I fucking know that I'm getting married? You don't think that I fucking know I was married when I met you? But do you know that I fell in love with you the first time I saw you. Every time you come around me; every time I feel like I have a chance with you, the timing is all wrong. Yeah I said it; I loved you the moment I saw you, I love you now and I can't help it. The emotions are so strong." Tears were now streaming down his face as he gripped his glass. "I just want you and only you, but now I have to choose. You are the only woman I've ever wanted to be with, to be faithful to, to live the rest of my life with; there would be no one else if I had you. You came back into my life right when I got the best job ever, the job that I could retire in and live comfortably, and earn a good reputation. But I just can't leave you alone and you can ruin me, and I will ruin you. Sometimes I think I'm willing to take the chance, sometimes I'm not." Mike spilled his guts all over the courtyard. "The question is will it be matters of the heart or what's supposed to matter in my life."

His words sent shockwaves through the air hitting me like a bullet. I slowly stumbled back and sat on the bench. He had said he loved me, but I never thought he was serious. I was happy with my children and the love of my life, but he was always that forbidden pleasure in the back of my mind. The fact that I never got him out of my system was more than just being dick whipped, perhaps it was something else. I knew it was more than just liquor talking and I knew Mike was and would always be nothing but trouble.

"What am I supposed to do with this? I refuse to let you ruin my life with your bullshit. You just want what you can't have! This is typical Mike. Oh, you willing to fuck my life up and move on. No, sir, not this time, I refuse." My words pissed Mike off.

"Oh, you just fucking dismiss me, Lee? You know I can tell Karl exactly how your pussy taste, exactly how it feels. Yea and that's post baby pussy, post married pussy." He gave a narcissistic chuckle.

"You threatening me, Mike? Well guess what… let me introduce you to the real fucking Leesha Renée. You fuck with my husband—my marriage—I will make sure you never fucking work as a corporate lawyer in San Antonio again. I will drag your name so far down in the mud you won't see the light of day. Oh, and trust and believe, I can handle my husband, but you, on the other hand, have always had a hard time handling your career. No one wants to hire a lawyer that fucks the client's wife. If I ain't got enough pull, Karl will definitely make sure your name is fucked. Try it and see. How would it feel, no career, no fiancé—all because you couldn't get over the taste and the feel of my pussy. Your choice, you wanna play or not? Ball is in your court." My eyes locked with Mike's, and we waged war with each other. He had pushed me in a corner, and I came out swinging.

"You would really take my career?" He shook his head. "All because I love you." Now he was backing off the cocky shit.

"Bitch, I will take your whole fucking life." I doubled down on my threat. Mike laughed and walked away. My heart was pounding out of my chest. I had talked so much shit, knowing I might not be able to back it up. I hoped Mike was done.

"Lee, I've been looking for you. Come in, we're taking pictures." Karl was walking toward me. I grabbed his hand, and we went inside. When Karl and I finally made it back to our table, I noticed Mike and his fiancé had left.

CHAPTER 13
Back to Normal

Karl and I were rekindling our life in every way. We actually fucked on the regular and he was home more. Our counseling sessions decreased to once every other week. Emotionally, I felt like a burden had been lifted after putting Mike in his place that night. After a few weeks with no word from him and some mentions of his name by Karl concerning business, I knew Mike was no longer a threat. I should have never let him touch me. Being unfaithful and sloppy had almost ruined my marriage.

I was sitting at my vanity applying lotion after my shower when Karl walked in.

"Hey, baby." He leaned down and kissed me.

"Hey, the kids sleep?" I asked.

"Yea, it was a struggle getting Kaiden down. He wanted to play dinosaurs all night." Karl massaged my shoulder. I leaned back, encouraging him to keep going. Instead, he gently kissed my neck, followed by a slow lick to my ear. I returned the affection with a kiss. He opened my cream-colored silk robe letting it fall to the ground. He got on his knees and started kissing and sucking my breasts. I stood up, and the sparkle in Karl's eye caused me to immediately get wet. He led me to the bed and turned me around. I positioned myself on my hands and knees, thinking he was going for a quickie. Instead, I felt him squeeze my ass, and opened me up, slowly licking my pussy from behind. My body trembled at the sensation of the gentle strokes from his tongue. Orgasm number one came slowly, painfully teasing me for more. He came up and entered me, satisfying the need to feel him inside of me. After a few strokes, Karl flipped the script, guiding me down on top of him placing me in the reverse cowgirl position. I quickly got over the disappointment of having to do the work, and slowly started to ride, gently rotating my hips just enough to make him weak.

"Oh, shit, baby, damn you feel so fuckin' good," he gasped.

"You like that, baby. You like how that pussy feel?"

"Fuck yes…Damn, slow down, shit." He begged for mercy.

"Naw, you wanted me up here, now sit back and enjoy the ride," I teased. Karl took a deep breath. I loved to drive him crazy like this. Finally, he decided to take back control and got me on my back, rocking me to ecstasy once again.

The next morning, we were awakened to a crash in the kitchen followed by a dramatic Lizzie scream. Karl and I ran to the kitchen to find Lizzie standing on the counter in a pink ballerina costume. There was a puddle of milk and a broken wine glass on the floor.

"What are you doing?" I yelled.

"Getting a glass of milk." My yelling caused her to cry hysterically.

"Why that glass, you don't drink milk from that. Where's your cup?" I asked. She pointed to Frankie sitting at the table, drinking milk from Lizzie's pink cup and eating a donut. Frankie was ignoring the whole scene like she didn't care she had her sister's favorite cup.

"Frankie! Why do you have her cup?"

"Because it's just a cup and I'm using it now." Frankie was making a habit out of purposely upsetting her sister.

"Give me the damn cup." I snatched it and threw it in the sink. Karl started cleaning the floor. Frankie did not flinch; she continued to eat her donut. "Lizzie, get your ass off that counter." I picked her up and sat her in the chair. "You know you don't drink from that kind of glass." I gave her some milk and followed Frankie's breakfast idea and handed her a donut. Then I went to check on Kaiden, who was already sliding out of his race car toddler bed. I took him to the restroom to clean up and put another pull up on. While I was stripping his urine-stained sheets off the bed, Karl walked in.

"I gotta go into the office today to catch up on things," he announced. My heartbeat became erratic then dropped to my stomach.

"On a Saturday? What do you mean catch up?" I turned toward him.

"Yea, there were a lot of problems this week and I was interrupted so much, my stuff didn't get done. I hate being behind at the beginning of the week," he explained.

"Is anyone else going into the office today?" I asked, stomach feeling uneasy.

"Not that I know of, there has been no overtime approved," he answered.

"Okay." I looked at his face, searching for any hint of deceit; the deceit that my stomach alerted me to.

"Alright, I'll try to hurry back and maybe we can take the kids to the zoo or something." He smiled.

"I don't think I'll be up to it after all three of them get done with me." I didn't return his smile. "The housekeeper is on vacation, and I have to at least get the kids' room, the bathrooms cleaned good."

"Okay, I'll see you later." He walked away.

Six hours later, Karl wasn't home yet. The kids finally went down for a nap, and I found a movie to watch and got a glass of wine. My mind wondered to Karl telling me he was going to the office. That was weird and my gut was telling me something wasn't right. But I had promised not to be so suspicious and accusatory. I also had to admit that my guilt of being with Mike made me leerier. So, I stayed tricking myself into thinking crazy.

* * *

I was already in bed, pretending to be sleep when Karl crept in the bedroom. He showered and slipped in bed. I laid there as still as possible and took a couple of loud breaths as if I were in a deep sleep. My gut spoke to me once again, but this time I was letting the universe reveal what I needed to know—no chasing, no guessing, and no pop-ups.

CHAPTER 14

The Deception Game

Karl slipped in and out of his old patterns. At the moment, Karl was back focusing on me and the kids, and I was becoming confident in our relationship again. The inconsistency did drive me crazy, but I took care of the kids and planned for Mikayla's destination wedding. I was looking forward to getting away, sitting on the beach, and drinking champagne. I planned for Mrs. Ruiz to watch the kids for the weekend while Karl and I attended the wedding in the Bahamas. I was still rushing around with two days to spare before we flew out. When I finally went to bed, I fell right asleep.

Strangely, I was awakened by a nightmare. It had been years since I had dreamed about my childhood and my dad. I checked my phone and had a DM alert. I opened up the message and was stunned when I saw Mike's name. **Game on,** with a laughing emoji flashed across my screen. My heart dropped as I recalled the last words I said to him,

"Your choice, you wanna play or not? Ball is in your court." *Shit! Did this asshole just circle the block to pay me back, to threaten me; Oh my God. This motherfucka' moving like he got nothing to lose.* This scared me. I physically reacted to the message, breaking out in a sweat. I didn't sleep anymore that night.

I walked around nervous every time Karl called my name. The guilt and threat of him finding out about Mike and me was kicking my ass. *Maybe I should confess and beg for forgiveness. Maybe I should wait till I actually catch Karl in whatever he's doing and drop the bomb…but what if there's nothing to catch right now?* My mind raced, trying to figure out how to get out of this mess. *Think, Leesha, there's gotta be a way out of this.* It came to me, the only way to possibly keep Karl from finding out was to meet with Mike. I had to figure out what to say to him. As of now he had the upper hand because it was obvious he didn't care about his career or pending marriage. Something happened and he was willing to throw all his cards on the table, but what? I poured me a whisky and coke and prepared to answer Mike.

What do you mean? I finally answered his DM. He did not respond. Three drinks in, I messaged him again. **Ok, let's meet up and talk.**

I'm done talking, I said all I needed to say to you, Mike finally responded.

What does game on mean, what you trynna say?

Ball's in my court, got it. He knew I was scared. That asshole would do anything for attention.

Ok. I called his bluff. I threw my phone down. He pissed me off, but I wasn't going to sit and beg.

Come over tomorrow. Hours later, he responded.

I'll be there at 10am. I was hoping I wasn't walking into a trap, but I doubted that Mike would pass up a chance to get me alone again. I had to be smart about this.

Ok, he responded.

Mike opened the door wearing sweatpants and a T-shirt. "Come in."

"Hello," I muttered.

"Have a seat. The last time we spoke it was quite heated," he continued.

"Yea, things got a little out of hand," I admitted.

"I can't believe you threatened me; that shit hurt me to the fuckin' core." He didn't waste time.

"You threatened to tell Karl about us, blowing up my whole damn marriage. I thought you would be better than that because I never did or said anything like that to you. Yea, we both are wrong and I'm so sorry about it, I regret all of this. But do I really deserve for you to tell my husband? You've been in my shoes."

"Yea, you're right. But I was mad. You were also right that I wanted something I couldn't have."

"When you messaged me, were you going to talk to Karl about us?"

"Yea. I'm taking a job in Dallas, and I was gonna tell him right before I left, just because."

"Just because you wanted to be an asshole?"

"No, because I was in my feelings, I told you I loved you and you fucking blew me off. But I'm over it now."

"So, are you gonna tell him or no?"

"Naw, I ain't worried about your marriage… but maybe you should be." He smirked.

"Believe me, I know what's going on in my marriage." I was curious but I didn't want to take the bait.

"Do you? Because if you did." He moved in closer. "If you did, I'd be fucking you right now." He ran his hand down the front of his pants. I rolled my eyes.

"Listen, what you and I did was wrong, it was always wrong. If you're trynna tell me Karl is fucking around with Rachel, well then, that's him. I got my own shit to answer for. Anyway, when are you moving?"

"In about a month."

"I'm surprised Karl hasn't mentioned anything," I said.

"No big deal. Me and him ain't cool like that. He doesn't care. He should be glad I'm leaving cause I was about to take his wife." There was no end to Mike's cockiness.

"Whatever. So, the Mrs. wants to move, too?"

"Yea, we both need a change. I got a good job there and she's applying to different positions. But I'm excited about leaving."

"Good for you. You leaving in peace, right?"

"Yea, no breaking up a seemingly happy home, but I did want to tell you goodbye."

"Well, goodbye and I really do wish you all the best." I walked to the door.

"Can I at least get a hug and a kiss?" he asked.

"No, Mike. Goodbye." I left.

Mike had thrown little crumbs to make me believe that Karl had something going on. I didn't respond in an effort to keep him out of my business once and for all. His comment did mess with me, but the truth would come to light soon enough.

When I got home, I finished packing and noticed that Karl had not even pulled out his suitcase. His outfit for the wedding was hanging on the door, but only because I put it there. We planned to fly out at 9 p.m. I called him to see if he was coming home early.

"Hey, babe, I noticed you're not packed. We're flying out for Mikayla's wedding tonight. Are you coming home early?"

"Yea, Lee, about that… I don't think I will be able to go. We are behind schedule on the new project and the buyer is acting crazy. People are working overtime, and I don't feel right just up and leaving," he explained.

"Karl, Mikayla is my friend, I've known her forever. You can't miss this. No, you are coming with me, this is not an option." I was beyond angry.

"She doesn't care if I'm there; you go. It will be fine. You can relax and have time away from the kids. This is not a bad thing; you need a break," he rationalized.

"No, don't try to make me believe this is a good thing, you're my husband and we had this planned. You can't just back out on me."

"Don't be dramatic, Lee."

"Don't you minimize my feelings. Okay, whatever you really got going on, make sure it's worth it." I hung up the phone and threw it across the bed. I took a deep breath to calm down. I needed to be good for Mikayla's wedding—be happy for her and not worried about my bullshit drama.

The kids had agreed to not fight. I had made a pot roast that would last a few days and made sure there were snacks. Mrs. Ruiz would still be spending the weekend at the house, and she brought her grandkids with her. The kids were excited to have company. I finished packing and left. Karl did not even come home to tell me goodbye.

When Mikayla asked about Karl, I told her he couldn't make it but sent his love. I made sure she didn't see any disappointment on me because it was her day, and happiness was the only vibe I wanted to bring. She had a beautiful beach wedding. She looked gorgeous in her flowy gown. After the wedding, I hung out with her cousins and danced all night. When I got back to my room, I showered and sat on the balcony with a bottle of wine. The weather was perfect and sitting there alone gave me some time to reflect on everything that had happened, and the part I played. No matter how hard I tried to stitch back our marriage, Karl seemed to think working on us was an option and not a necessity. He had not even called to check on me. I picked up my phone and checked the outside cameras. Karl's truck was home, but that still didn't mean he wasn't out. I checked the cameras in the house, and it was dark. Karl and I didn't have a camera in our room, but I checked the kids, and they were all asleep in the girls' room.

The next day, I enjoyed a nice breakfast and had a ninety-minute massage at the spa. I met up with the cousins again and chilled by the pool for the rest of the day. One thing Karl was right about, I did need some time alone. How long was I going to sit around and wait to figure out what was going on with him? Was my guilt causing me to sit by idly and let him tear me down emotionally? Was I subconsciously punishing myself for my indiscretions? All this was exhausting. First, Mike was playing games to get attention and now Karl being deceptive. I was so done with his shit.

CHAPTER 15

Final Decisions

"I know you're angry," Karl said as I threw my suitcase on the floor.

"How do you know? I haven't even talked to you. You did not even call to say anything. It is obvious you don't care anymore. It's obvious you would rather be somewhere else, with someone else. At this point I don't care. You don't care and neither do I."

"I care, I'm just trying to keep my family's company alive," he protested.

"Karl, get real, the company is not in jeopardy. You all are wealthy, and you got contracts for the next eight years at least."

"Contracts that can be taken away if I don't conduct business correctly now!"

"I asked for a weekend, Karl. You couldn't put me first for one weekend?"

"I know and I'm sorry I missed the wedding."

"It's not the wedding, it's you disappointing me over and over."

"Okay, I get it and I'm sorry."

"Why don't you be straight with me. Are you seeing someone? Are you still fucking my sister or is it Rachel?"

"No! We don't talk anymore and no again to Rachel."

"I want to know what's really going on. Who are you seeing," I spoke softly because I was done being angry.

"No one, there is no one, I promise," he said.

"Okay, I choose to trust you." I was tired of going in circles.

I started to spend my time fundraising for school field trips and organizing the PTA at the girls' school. I had to stay busy. I also worked with Kaiden, trying to get him to talk. I loved hanging out with the kids. Karl avoided working weekends, but still came home late sometimes. I didn't even care anymore. He mentioned they were having a going-away luncheon for Mike, but I declined the invitation. I wanted to stay away from that office, Mike, and Rachel. She had been crossing my mind a lot lately. Ever since I caught Karl with Leanna, it seemed like I had almost forgotten about Rachel. But now, I was becoming paranoid about her presence again.

I had just gotten home from the girl's school when my phone rang.

"Lee, we are having the luncheon today for Mr. Sinclair. The food was ordered, but we forgot cake. Can you run to that bakery you like and pick out one, we have a lot of people coming." Karl sounded stressed.

"I just got home and I'm a mess. I helped make tie-dye shirts for girls' track and field. I got dye all over me still. Can't you have Rachel go get your cake; ain't that her job, to do whatever you need?" I couldn't hold back my sarcasm.

"I'm asking you to, my wife. Besides, she's busy decorating," he shot back.

"Sure, your wife will be happy to be her back-up… after all I've been her back-up all this time." I hung up the phone.

Be here by 1:00 and leave the attitude at home. Karl sent a text. I didn't respond. I had every right to have an attitude. I was mentally and sexually frustrated; it had been weeks since he had even tried to touch me.

I showered, straightened my hair, and put on a black maxi dress that showcased my curves. At the bakery, I selected two cakes and had 'We Will Miss You' on one and 'New Job, New Adventure' on the other. I pulled up to the front of the building just in time to see Mike and his fiancé walking in.

"Hi." I waved. Mike walked over and she followed.

"Hello, Lee, umm Mrs. Michaels," he said. She glared at him.

"Mr. Sinclair, sorry to hear you're leaving. I'm sure you're gonna do great. How are you?" I acknowledged his fiancé.

"I'm fine." She smiled.

"Let me help you," Mike said, grabbing one of the cakes.

"Thank you." We got in the elevator, and I felt her staring at me, which made me nervous.

When the elevator opened, the conference room was right in front of us. Rachel was the first person I saw. She rushed over and took the cake from me.

"Thank you so much. I was too busy to get the cake," she said.

"You're welcome, I'm happy to help," I answered, making sure my attitude was still at home. I left the conference room and headed to Karl's office. He was walking out.

"Hey, Lee, I'm going to the conference room, we're getting started. You look beautiful by the way," he said, admiring the fitted dress.

"Thank you, maybe you can see what's under here after the party." I smiled.

"I'd like that." He winked at me.

The luncheon was nice, everyone wished Mike well and offered unsolicited advice. His fiancé stayed attached to his side and I stayed away. He wouldn't stop staring at me and I tried to ignore him. My body did react to his eyes, but I knew better to get dragged into that mess again. Rachel and Karl didn't go near each other, and it was obvious it was because I was there. They acted so awkward, but maybe it was because I was known to make a scene when it came to them. I was embarrassed about my past behavior.

My phone dinged as soon as I got in my car.

I'm leaving, you'll never see me again, come over, I wanna see you one last time. Please say yes. It was Mike.

I immediately typed **No,** but didn't send it. I remembered he still could tell Karl if I pissed him off enough. So, I didn't respond at all. Maybe I should have because once again Karl didn't touch me that night. I was at a loss. What could I do to save this marriage. I was tired of sitting back waiting for him to make a move. I was tempted to get at Mike for one last time. Mike must of knew he was on my mind.

Please, let's meet up at the coffee spot. He was persistent.

One cup, that's it, I responded, knowing I was about to get myself in trouble.

Ok, one cup. I promise.

It was inevitable that Mike once again talked me into going to his place. He poured me some whisky, surely trying to strip me of any guard I had up. Three drinks in and my head was swimming. I moaned, gripping the pillow as Mike insatiably ate my pussy.

"Damn, you taste so fucking good." He gripped my thighs tighter as I came. He sat up, stroking his hard dick, then slid a condom on. He lifted my thighs and slid in, making my body tremble. He rocked me into another orgasm. "That's right, baby, cum on that dick one more time," he groaned. His hand suddenly came down slapping my thigh as his pace increased, generating his orgasm. Both of us passed out.

"What the fuck is this!" I heard a woman scream. Mike's fiancé snatched the covers off of us. "I knew you was fucking my man. Mike, how could you do this? Why?" He jumped up and pulled on his pants and I was already up throwing on my clothes.

"Sasha! I'm sorry, calm down," he said. I said nothing. I just got my ass out of there; I looked back and saw Mike holding her to keep her from coming after me.

I sat at the kitchen table waiting for Karl to come home. My chest ached and I felt like I had the weight of the world on me. Every time I looked at the kids, tears fell. I had fucked up and knew it was a matter of time before Karl found out. Just as I expected, the front door opened, and he walked in. He saw the distraught look on my face and just shook his head. I swallowed the lump in my throat.

"You're home early," I spoke.

"I'm sure you were expecting me," he answered, throwing his keys on the counter.

"Yes, I was," I mumbled.

He hit the table and got in my face; I tried to catch my breath as the tears started to fall.

"You just couldn't stay away from him, could you?" he yelled. I said nothing. "His woman came to my office, screaming that Mike just got done fucking you," he said. I just sat there shaking and crying. "I could kill you! Stop crying because I don't care about your fucking tears!" He yelled so loud I thought I heard the walls shake.

"I'm sorry, it just happened, I didn't mean it to." I finally was able to speak.

"No, it didn't just happen, Lee… you been fucking him."

"No, that's not true, Karl. I'm sorry. You never touch me, and I just got lonely."

"I never touch you? Like I said, you been fucking him." I gasped at his words, but then went in defensive mode.

"Well, if it isn't faithful, honest Karl. Yes, the man who was caught at a hotel with his wife's sister; the one who has been coming home late, and the one who used to sniff so far up Rachel's ass he couldn't see straight. I made a mistake, and I am owning up to it, but when are you gonna own up to yours?" I yelled back.

"Never! It's over." He walked out. Just like that, my marriage ended.

EPILOGUE

"Kaiden get off the game and get ready, your dad will be here soon to pick y'all up," I yelled.

"Oh sh.." Kaiden moaned. "I just got killed. Damn, I'm gonna get my stuff now." At the age of thirteen, he tested my patience.

"Watch your mouth before I knock your lips off, boy. I told you about that." I snatched the controller out his hand.

"Sorry, Momma," he said.

"Frankie, are you ready?" I asked. She was in her standard sweat suit and hair in a puffy ponytail.

"I been ready." She pointed to her suitcase by the door.

"Lizzie are you ready," I yelled into the room, knowing she was not.

"Almost, but I'm not taking that ugly ski suit Dad bought. He could've saved his money on that," Lizzie complained.

"Now, how are you going to ski without it? Put it in your suitcase. I ain't playing around with you." I was already getting irritated with her.

"Black people don't ski anyway," she mumbled. I gave her a warning look. "Okay, I'll pack it."

Frankie got up and went to the kitchen to check the food my mom was cooking for Christmas. She had moved in with us after James passed away a year ago.

"OOOHH, everything smells so good! I wanna stay here with you and Grandma, cause y'all about to eat good," she said. "We gonna be eating season-free, tasteless Momma Rachel food." Frankie rolled her eyes.

"Y'all should be used to her cooking by now," I said, thinking back how I found out she and Karl had been having an affair before Kaiden was even born. And I thought I ruined the marriage; a woman's intuition never lies. Oh well, the kids were teenagers now and that was old news.

There was a knock at the door, and I opened it to see Karl and Rachel standing there. She still couldn't make eye contact with me after all these years. Karl was getting more and more handsome as time went on, but Rachel looked older than me. The fact that I still looked good, now better than her, secretly made me happy.

"Hello and Merry Christmas," I greeted them.

"Hello Lee, Merry Christmas," he said, giving me a hug.

"Kids, Dad's here, time to go," I said.

"Coming!" they all yelled.

After a lot of running back and forth and goodbyes, the kids were gone, and the house was quiet. Mom poured us some egg nog and we sat down to watch movies. The Christmas tree sparkled in the corner, demanding our attention. We both sat there looking at it, remembering when all we had was each other and a small Christmas tree. The more things changed, the more they stayed the same.

LETTER FROM THE AUTHOR

Thank you for reading *The Betrayal of Lee*, the final book in the Lee Series. This brutally honest story is a depiction of how the roles we play fail to change the core of ourselves. Leesha and Karl's marriage is one of happiness and hope, but their individual wants and needs eventually overpowers the previous urge to be the perfect partner. Leesha and Karl fall short of mutual expectations which causes them to live with secrets instead of bringing them to the forefront to be reconciled. This is the story of many marriages, but more importantly this is the story of a woman still learning to trust herself while making mistakes along the way.

My goal was to demonstrate how emotions can easily lead us astray and magnify the separation between our actions and our true selves. While the mistakes exemplified are avoidable and open for judgement, I trust readers to respond with the compassion and understanding that we all hope for in our times of confusion and turmoil.

Jennifer Janell

I hope you enjoyed *The Betrayal of Lee*, and the other two books in the Lee Series. I pray you see a little of yourself or have developed some understanding of what others may go through when faced with motherhood and an imperfect marriage.

Jennifer Janell